RAIN RISING

Courtne Comrie

HARPER
An Imprint of HarperCollins*Publishers*

Library of Congress Cataloging-in-Publication Data
Names: Comrie, Courtne, author.
Title: Rain rising / Courtne Comrie.
Description: First edition. | New York, NY : HarperCollins Publishers,
    [2022] | Audience: Ages 8-12. | Audience: Grades 4-6. | Summary:
    Thirteen-year-old Rain, who struggles with low self-esteem, must
    overcome sadness after her older brother Xander is severely beaten
    up at a frat party, but through the help of an after-school circle
    group, Rain finds the courage to help herself and her family heal.
Identifiers: LCCN 2021057325 | ISBN 9780063159730 (hardcover)
Subjects: CYAC: Novels in verse. | Self-esteem—Fiction. | Families—
    Fiction. | Hate crimes—Fiction. | Self-help groups—Fiction.
    African Americans—Fiction. | LCGFT: Novels in verse.
Classification: LCC PZ7.5.C67 Rai 2022 | DDC [Fic]—dc23
LC record available at https://lccn.loc.gov/2021057325

Typography by Carla Weise
22 23 24 25 26   PC/LSCH   10 9 8 7 6 5 4 3 2 1
❖
First Edition

This book is dedicated to
Mommy Tetlah, Lisa, Toni,
Julanie, Savannah, and GG.
I love you guys so much.
And to you—yes, you, reader.
This one is for you, too.

1. JUST RAIN

"Rain!"
Mom's voice shakes me up like
the roll of thunder
each morning.

But *my name isn't as cool as it sounds.*
Mom could've been more creative when naming me.
Like
Rayne
Reine
or Raayn.
Nope   just Rain.
Like wet weather, as if
Mom was heavy on some
nursery rhyme stuff.

Down came the RAIN and washed the spider out,
RAIN RAIN go away,
or maybe that soul-stirring

Lord RAIN down on us at every Sunday morning service.
I groan a bit until I finally
open my eyes to a deep gray.
The sun no longer peeks through my room
like a nosy neighbor,
because it's the middle of winter.

So I drag myself out of bed, stand in front of my mirror,
                                    and a sadness
                             that *same* sadness
                 the sadness that's so hard to escape from
starts boiling up inside me like hot water.

            "Rain!" Mom calls again, and
I know this is my final warning.
            "Okay, Mommy, I'm up!" I yell back,
unsure
because   in reality
I'm feeling *down* at the sight of myself   in the
      mirror.

I squeeze the fat on my arms   and sigh.
I guess you can't pray yourself skinny or pretty.
I pull the fat on my cheekbones   snapping it back
            like putty.
            "I'm coming," I whisper to myself, in the
                  hope that I'm *going,*

despite how stuck I feel
in this body,
            my mood
falling   just like the   rain.
I guess Mom did name me right after all.

2. RELEASING MY GRIP

I walk out of my room
and bang on the bathroom door
like there's a fire.
            "Come on, X, hurry up!"
I'm so tired   and X always takes so   l o n g.
The door swings open and
Xander walks out in his   crisp white-and-khaki
    uniform   brushing the sides of
his faded high-top, which Willie the barber *always*
    finesses.

        "Looking this good ain't easy, Rain." He
            smiles his wide smile.

I look up at his tall self
roll my eyes
try to push him   out of the way with all my
     might.
Xander is real strong.
          "Okay, okay, you got it, Rain-drop." He laughs.
I laugh too,   releasing my grip from his arms.
We do this every morning.
X always makes me feel better when I feel

                                        stuck.

3. IN THE BATHROOM

As I brush my teeth my mind is filled with these
     thoughts,
thoughts   that even the water can't drown out.

You're ugly.
You're not good enough.
You're worthless.
Nobody likes you.
Only bad things will happen.

Sometimes this sadness in me that
I can't   shake off
this fog in my mind,
              sometimes it just comes and I don't know
                   why.

No one knows about it but me,
so instead I just keep saying to myself,
Snap out of it, Rain.

4. XCEPTIONAL X

Mom has breakfast made but
Xander has no time   for sit-down time,
                              he never does.
Mom doesn't always have time to make breakfast
since she works *two* jobs
at *two* different places,
because she's got to support the *two* of us.

So I sit at the kitchen table
eating eggs

                                          scrambled.
Mom starts.
        "You got your keys, X?"
        "Yeah, Ma, you got your bag?"
     I bite into my bacon as I watch my big brother.
Xander
aka X
aka Xceptional X
aka Xcellent X
the best X-ample
who's *low-key a hero* in my   City.
Taller than Mom
and Dad,
though I sometimes forget how tall Dad is.
The brown-skin athlete with the faded high-top
       with all that Black-boy joy

                                          Xander.
Everybody and their mommas love

                                          Xander.
Who was an honors student at *my* school
         his *old* school
         City Middle School
with straight As and a heart of gold.

Who plays
every sport well and is   cool with every teacher
                             cool with every student
                             cool with every person you find
standing on any block   in my City.
So of course
it was a no-brainer
that for high school   *he'd* get a full scholarship
to the private and super-duper expensive
Elite Preparatory Academy,
which is nowhere near our City.
Not many Xanders   exist there.
              But at least one does,   Mom says.

To be on time for school
Xander catches the six forty-five a.m. train
                                  the good train
for a whole *hour* ride   in a uniform without creases.
Mom makes sure he looks good
when he steps out of our house,
because like she says,
not many get to step out, and when they do,
they don't always make it back   the same.

              "Later, Rain."
Xander wraps his long arm around my neck

7

I lean into it   wishing he could walk me to school,
the way he used to.
          "Later, X."

Mom kisses both of our cheeks,
then holds on to our shoulders with her eyes closed for
      a few seconds,
and X and I know she's saying a quick prayer.
          "Bye, babies, love y'all."
          "Love you too, Ma."
          "Bye, Mommy, love you."
And they're gone before I finish my breakfast.

5. TIMES LIKE THESE

I take Nara's shortcut to school,
but this year I'm walking by myself
because
Nara's parents bought a house
                    bought a *whole* house
on the north side of the City.

She can only get a ride from her parents or Uber to get
     to school now,
and it sucks because it's
our last year at City Middle School.

I'm wearing Xander's old hoodie under Xander's old
     jacket,
winter boots   book bag heavy on my back
                              walking through old dirty snow
in the coldness of winter.

Mom can't afford to buy me a monthly bus pass,
thanks to the price of X's train tickets.
So I hum songs to pass the time instead.

Right before I walk into
City Middle School,
I take out my cell phone and put the camera close to my
     face
to see how my hair looks   *sigh*.
I'm so frustrated at how my edges don't
silk, smooth, swirl, or cooperate.
I try to brush them down
with the palm of my hand but   nothing.

So instead I reach for my black headband
from the side of my book bag
                    for times like these
and put it on instead
because edges are a big deal.

6. COOL WITH IT

"Rain!"
I walk into school and head straight into
the cafeteria and see Nara at our usual table, waving
    me over,
surrounded by people,   of course,   a crowd.

"Hey, Nara!"
I wave   but I feel nervous,
aware   of my outfit
        how I don't have a lot, so I'm always in X's old hoodies,
aware   of my body
            how much bigger it seems than everybody else's,
more aware   of my hair
            how it isn't as curly and long as Nara's.

But I pretend like I'm okay,
because *nobody is allowed to clown me.*

Because since pre-K
I've been known as   *Nara's best friend.*
I'm cool with it because Nara's
so pretty   so cool   so popular.
I walk over and sit on top of the table the way she does,
even though I know security doesn't like it.
Mom would give me   *the look*   for sure.

I scoot real close to Nara, so my thighs don't touch
     anyone else.
               "Wassup, Rain?"
Dante's got his arm around Nara's back.

I smile
probably harder than I should.
               "Hey, Dante."
He's not hearing me.
He's stuck like glue to Nara,
whose family thought it was cute for her
to have a boyfriend in eighth grade.   *Shaking my head.*

Mom would *freak out* if she *ever* found out,
so I never say nothing and never will,
but I *do* notice Dante's and Nara's matching sneakers.

And how good his olive-green hoodie looks
against his cocoa-brown skin.

Dante's best friend   Amare   comes up to the table
and gives me a quick hug because
hugs are like *hellos*   especially since
I've known him forever, since both our families go to
    Hope Church.
His mom and mine are friends.
            "Hey, Amare," I say, my eyes still stuck on
                    Nara and Dante.
            "How's it going, Rain?"
I look up at Amare, who has those expensive
    headphones around his neck
like a necklace
like a scarf
like a badge of honor. *I guess he's really got money.*
            "I'm good . . . nice headphones."
            "Yeah, my pops got them for me."
            "That's wassup."
He nods   proud.
I almost wince at the thought of my mom spending
    money like that
on me.
            That could *never* happen.

He goes up and daps Dante.
Then he hugs Nara, who hugs him a bit tight for
somebody with a *whole* boyfriend.
I know I won't be getting Nara's attention anytime
    soon,
so I reach into my book bag
for my English class reading.

The bell rings and I'm shaken out of my book.
Everyone is heading out,
and while I'm gathering my things
Nara leaves with Dante without me,
                without saying goodbye
or maybe I just didn't hear it.
       "You good, Rain?" Amare is in front of me
        again.
       "Yeah, thanks. I'm cool."

7. I WALK INTO ENGLISH CLASS

Excited because Miss Walia is my favorite teacher in
    this school,
and English is my favorite subject *besides the end of the
    very last period.*
Because   *to be honest*
it's the furthest thing from a *math equation*—
science irks my *DNA*,
history goes *past me.*
But give me a book,   a poem,   let me
write an essay and I'm good.
English class gives my feelings   my thoughts   their
    own home

                                    a sort of place to belong.
In class discussions,
it's always a
            how do you feel about this?
Or a
            why did you think the writer did this?
Like
what I think   matters   here.

"Hello, class."
Miss Walia is her usual smiles
wearing her City Middle School hoodie
with her hair in a loose bun.

I sit in my seat next to Nara.
"You left me this morning," I whisper loud enough for
    her to hear.
She looks at me with her mouth forming an O.
    Fake shocked. I know it.
"My bad, girl, you know Dante," she laughs.
Not really   but I laugh anyway because
Nara's so silly   and I mean   she's my best
    friend   after all.
Miss Walia begins handing out sheets of paper and
    stops at my desk.
"Good morning, Nara, Rain."
"Hi, Miss Walia." I smile.
I look at Nara, who rolls her eyes.

I laugh and shake my head because
Nara never likes the things I like.

8. WHEN WE WERE YOUNGER

Nara would tell me,
"Rain, don't be afraid, you can do it!"
When she'd see me go still on the top of the jungle gym
or tense up in large crowds at the school fairs,
or keep my mouth closed when our kindergarten
    teacher asked me
        the color
        the shape
        the answer to what *that* plus *that* equaled.

She'd say,
"Come *on*, Rain!"
And because of her
I'd eventually do it   until
    it became me doing all the things *she'd* want to do.

I couldn't tell the difference between what I'd want to do
versus
what Nara could get me to do.

But without her I'd be afraid of most things.

I needed her so much.

9. IT'S NIGHTTIME

I'm lying down on my bed with my homework,
                              home alone
waiting for Xander to come from his school workouts.
I stare at the ceiling
                 my heart racing.

                                        You're ugly.
                              You're not good enough.
                                     You're worthless.
                                   Nobody likes you.
                            Only bad things will happen.
I hate being home alone.
Especially when the thoughts get too heavy for me.
I'm wondering
what it'd be like if I
just wasn't here anymore.

I'm dreading
having to see people tomorrow
at school
again.

I jump up at the sound of the front door   *shook.*
        "Xander?"
I jump off the bed as if the sheets have become   hot
    coal.
        "Rain?"
        "Mom?"
I run into the living room to see
Mom sitting on the sofa   taking off her work sneakers.
I jump on the sofa   nearly crushing her.
"Mommy!"
I wrap my arms around her.
I don't always get to see her   before I fall asleep   or
    after I get up.
This is a surprise
            but a good one
                        one worth staying around for.
"Rain." She kisses my cheek,
and I feel safe and sad   and want to fall asleep right
    here right now   with my mom
although I'm thirteen,
although I should grow up,

but right now
I don't
                want to.

Mom leans back into the sofa with her eyes closed and
    exhales deeply.
I watch her hair
                        curl around her round brown face
her skin a lighter brown than X and me
almost caramel   sticky with sweat   and hard work.

She smiles and opens her eyes.
The front door opens to Xander, who looks   *exhausted*
from workouts with his team.
"What y'all doin' up?" he asks,
dropping his book bag and duffel bag on the floor.
"It's called quality time?" I tease.
"Oh, word? Let me get some of that too."
He jumps into the middle of the sofa
    right in between   Mom and me
and although Mom's already fallen asleep
and Xander will eventually get up,

I almost forget how sad I've been feeling.

10. WHEN WE WERE YOUNGER

Mom would have Xander studying every night
even if he didn't have a test,
and I would just watch while I colored.
"Life is the *real* test," she would say tiredly, leaning over
    his shoulder.
I never knew what she meant by that,
but would color slower when she'd say it.

"Ma." X would push his books across the table,
or across his bed
or across the floor   depending on where he was
    studying.
"Ma," he'd start again, slightly turning to me for some
    type of mutual support. "I can't do this."
"*Can't?*"
Mom didn't like us using the word   *can't*,
especially Xander.
"*Ma*," he'd whine.
"Xander." She'd pause. "You have to be better than me."

Better than Mommy?   I'd wonder, because who could
     be better than her?
I love Mommy.

I'd scrunch my face up
shading in the flower   the sun   the clouds
with the colors that weren't broken all the way.
Even though I'd often force those ones to color
     too   the way
Mom forced Xander to study.
"Okay," X would say,   and   reopen his books.
After a while
he stopped saying   *can't*

                                        entirely.

11. WHICH SIDE OF THE TRACKS

It's after school the next day and
Nara pays for an Uber for us
to get to my house.
"I use Uber so much that I get a discount now, Rain!"
And now she's barely paying attention to her homework

as we sit with our books around my table,
because she shrieks under her breath.
"Zach is so *fine!*"
I lift my head from my notes and look into the living
    room
at Xander and Zach,
who is his closest friend from his private school   but
boys like Zach are barely found in this City.

                                    Nara's right.
Zach looks just like one of those actors
                                    on TV
                                    in the movies
                                     on magazine covers
with blond hair and green eyes   looking like a
Matt-something
Leonardo-something
Brad-something.
Sometimes I just want to touch him to see if he's *real.*
I'm sure
people say the same thing about Xander,
but Zach is basically X
dipped in white icing.
Although some people would say
they're nothing alike based on the outside.
"He's a senior . . . in *high* school, Nara."
"And?"

I shake my head at Nara.

Although she's thirteen, she could pull off being   older,
and I'm sure Zach would give a girl like her the time of
   day.

Nara's   skin is bright caramel   light brown eyes
      clear knees
nice smile   hair that curls   and slim thick
unlike me
            whose skin is darker than milk chocolate
            even darker knees
            eyes too dark to be a color
            hair that puffs all the way out
            legs full of battle scars
            from trying to be
         just as strong   just as fast   just as capable
                              as Xander.

And just *thick* thick.

"*College* visit?"

Nara gets up from the table and goes over to the sofa.

"Yeah." X stands from the living room sofa and stretches,
his fingertips almost hitting the ceiling.

"We're going next week. Elite Prep is sponsoring a
   visit there. It's a trip for juniors, but seniors who've
   applied there are allowed to go check it out. We'll
   be staying in the dorms and everything. Zach and I
   applied but haven't visited yet."

I walk over.

"Where?"

"Smith University." He waves the college pamphlet in
the air.

I raise my eyebrows.

"That's a good school."

Nara sits on the arm of the sofa that's closest to Zach.

"You're going too?" she asks,

leaning real close to him,   the back of her crop
top rising all the way up.

"Of course!"

Xander walks over to the kitchen table and looks at my
homework.

"Where's your math?"

Sigh.

He *knows* me.

He *knows* I won't do it.

I walk over to the kitchen table and pull the homework
out from under my notebooks.

"I don't get it."

He looks at me and smiles.

"Solve for *x*? This is *easy*. Come on, Rain-drop." He sits
and I sit with him.

Xander is what people would call a   scholar-athlete.

Football his favorite sport   math his best subject.

I squint at him as he looks at the problems.

Shaking my head.

Dude is so focused that
sometimes I can't tell which side of the
tracks he came from
for real   for real.

12. LATER THAT NIGHT

I catch X looking at that college pamphlet in his
bedroom.
"How many times are you going to look at it?" I tease.
He laughs,   kind of.
I open my mouth to speak, but he turns to me and asks,
"You cool?"
I ignore his question and snatch the pamphlet from his
hand.
"Let me guess." I smile. "The best football team to play
on?"
He shrugs. "I guess."
I guess?
"You—"
"I guess," he interrupts me. "I guess that's what people
would want. For me to play there."

"That'll be *so* dope." I look at the pamphlet
at the big dorms   at the lush grass
the buffet-style cafeteria   the *dining halls*.
"Yeah, but—"
The front door closes and Xander jumps up, grabs the
     pamphlet, and runs out the room.
"Yo, Ma! Look where I'm going!"

13. THE NEXT MORNING

Mom wakes me up a bit earlier
to do my hair.
"I wish my hair was thick like yours, Rain."
I can hear the smile in her voice   although
my hair is often a pain for me to   manage.

"Do you know how nice your hair is? Feel it? Beautiful
     and healthy."
"Yes, Mommy, I know."
I lean my head down on the kitchen table as she's
     deciding.

"How about I cornrow it and in a couple of weeks you
     can take it out and wear it that way too?"
"Ehh . . ."
"Cornrows into a puff?"
I nod.
She hums a church song as she braids.

Xander walks into the kitchen as Mom is finishing my
     hair.
"Ma, what it take for you to doll me up the way you do
     Rain?"
I laugh. Mom laughs too.
Xander always makes us laugh.
"Boy, don't even start . . ."
Mom sprays my head with sheen spray,
marking the completion of my hairstyle.
"Go look."
I get up and run into the bathroom   look into the
     mirror   immediately
I'm in love with my hair   the braids   how it shapes
     my face
the perfect position of the puff.
I smile.
"Yeah, sis." X walks in and daps me up. "Looking good."
I nod in agreement, although I'm starting to feel

                                             unsure.

14. BARELY LOOK

After lunch I
go with Nara, who wants to meet
her other friends
Tiffany and Julie
in the girls' bathroom.
The four of us avoid class and
stand in front of the mirror,   *which I don't like.*
But Nara grabs my hand like we're in second grade
      again and says,
"Please, Rain."

I nod and stay
and watch them
apply lip gloss and mascara
that I don't think anyone really notices.   *Who knows.*
I wash my hands in the meantime.
"Look at how *fat* I'm getting."
Julie lifts her shirt and pinches
the one inch of fat on her stomach.
"Ugh. Same."

Tiffany brushes the long brown
extensions in her hair,   which makes me think my
     hair
is not as great.

Nara is taking mirror pics and says,
"Thank *God* it's winter and I've got my color back. I get
     too dark in summer."
"Exactly."
"Same."
I bite my lip.
"True," I say, although I'm
dark all the time.

I'm just the wrong shade of brown.

I barely look at the mirror as the water runs through
     my fingers.

15. SOME TEACHERS

Some teachers
do the *most.*
Too much   too extra.
Some in good ways   some in bad ways   but
Miss Walia does the *most* in good ways   *always.*
She's the teacher who randomly brings cookies during
   a test
decorates her classroom for the holidays   and even
puts the occasional smiley-face sticker on top of your
   essay.
According to some kids   including Nara   it's
   corny
but Miss Walia doing these things gives me
something to look forward to   especially on my
   saddest days.

"Everybody, everybody." Miss Walia claps her hands
   together, smiling wide.
Today her hair is out and it's long, dark, and silky.
I wonder if she ever needs to brush it

or if it just comes out
perfect like that.
She has us answering a short response,
but now we're all looking up at her.
"I have a little surprise for you all."
She opens her closet door to a large pile of
what look like orange notebooks.

    "Journals!"

My eyes widen.   I really like the orange and
I've never used a journal before.
"Erin and Keon, can you help me pass them out?"
Keon drops a journal on my desk.
I run my hand over the soft yet hard exterior.
    I open it.   I close it.
It even smells fresh.
I look over at Nara, who continues working on her
    short response   unbothered.
"They're yours," Miss Walia continues. "You can use
    them for anything. I use a journal myself. How
    about for the first entry, you all list three things
    that have made you smile today? You all can try that
    out if you'd like."
"Thank you, Miss Walia."
"Thank you, miss."
"Thank you."
"Appreciate it."

"Thank you," I whisper, flipping through the pages
    again.
The bell rings   and I pack my bag
as I follow Nara out.
    I look back and notice that she left her orange journal
                                    on her desk.
            "See you tomorrow, Rain." Miss Walia smiles
            at me.

16. CHECK MY GROOVE

Mom's working late   again,
which makes my stomach hurt,
but X is in charge of dinner and makes
his special spaghetti with
ketchup and black pepper.

"Rain, Rain, check this!"
I turn around in my seat at
the kitchen table
to see X putting a small piece of lettuce
on top of my plate of his special spaghetti.

"Like them fancy restaurants. I call this five-star!"
I laugh.
"I call it *pathetic*."
"Yeah aiight, you're just a hater."
He puts the plate in front of me
and goes into the living room.

"What do you eat at your fancy school?" I call out.
　　"Lobster?"
He shakes his head.
"Not even close."
I roll my eyes.
"Yeah right. With *that* tuition, I'm sure Muffy and Buffy
　　get the caviar out."

I start to eat and X walks over
with a speaker in one hand,
his phone in the other. "Come on, Rain."
　　　　　　"So, you're not eating?" I look over at his
　　　　　　untouched plate.
He puts his phone down and stuffs a fork full of
　　spaghetti into his mouth.
I shake my head and smile.
　　　　　*X is always clowning.　　Always making me
　　　　　　forget how sad I feel.*
He puts the speaker down on the table.

Out comes some old-school
Sam Cooke–sounding music.

He starts shuffling back and forth.
"Check my groove, Rain-drop."
I laugh with my mouth full.
He stretches out his long arms.
"Come on, come on."
I get up and we're both dancing and moving,
laughing and pretending
we're in some movie,
or at some family reunion
with a soul train line.
            "Ayeee, get it."
I cheer us on.
X does a spin and moonwalks into   the sofa.
            "Ouch!"
We laugh.
The door opens.
            "What's this?"
Mom walks in and X goes and grabs her,
and now they're dancing and laughing.
X switches the music to Afrobeat
hip-hop
salsa
jazz

just about anything to keep us
moving.

"Okay, Rain, take it easy on us!" he shouts as I dance.
He knows I love a good beat.
Mom's clapping and moving her shoulders   in some
   shimmy.
            X and I try to do the same.
            "Okay, Ma, I see you." X laughs,
and I'm laughing
and I'm hoping
that
this night will never
end.

17. THAT NIGHT BEFORE BED

I try to write in the journal   something
anything   but the pages are just so crisp   that
    I'm afraid to ruin it
with my handwriting.
So instead   I just lay it down in bed with me   for
    a bit   until I finally crack it open:

Three Things That Made Me Smile Today:
1) Getting this journal from Miss Walia that she
   said we can use for anything.
2) Xander's famous spaghetti for dinner.
3) Dancing with Mommy and Xander in the living
   room. A lot of people don't know this about me,
   but I love to dance or do some type of movement
   to a good beat. Maybe one day I can do more of
   that.

I look down at what I wrote and reread it a million
    times.

It looks good   it makes me smile   and I can't
wait to write in my journal

again.

18. WHEN WE WERE YOUNGER

Xander was always trying to do something
experimental with food.
"How about with cereal?" He lined up three different
types of cereal on the kitchen table.
"Cereal?" I dipped my hands in the frosted ones,   my
favorite.
"Yeah, Dad would"—he smacked my hand away from
out the cereal box—"Dad would always bake
something with cereal. What do you think? Rice
Krispies Treats?"
Dad would. Dad would. Dad would.
All he spoke about was *Dad.*
I couldn't remember memories with Dad as much as he
could.
"Oh, plus he got me this!" Xander reached into a plastic
bag and pulled out a speaker.

"To play music?" I asked, although I was more
　　　concerned about the Rice Krispies Treats.
"Yup." He smiled. "Dad loves music."
I nodded　　　　sort of remembering that he did
kind of.
　　　　"Oh."

19. CAVITY

I guess some could say I have
a telephone dad.
I don't see Dad a whole lot
once　　　　a　　　　year
maybe.
He makes two calls every month　　　*if he doesn't forget.*
One for me.
One for Xander.
　　　　"How's my Ray Ray doing?"
It's *my* turn and
he's the only one who　　　*ever*　　　calls me
Ray Ray.
　　　　"I'm good."

My voice is real tight
because
Mom gives me the phone   even though I waved my
     hands
in the air

                         asking her
                         to tell him

                                        I'm asleep
                                        I'm in the shower
                                        I'm dead.

But Mom never listens.
Even though
every call is like getting a
                         cavity filled in.
It's
supposed to help but
it still

                                                  hurts.

20. XANDER'S CAVITY

As soon as X comes in from school   the phone rings
    and it's Dad.

          "Damn it," X says under his breath.
I smile because I hear it   and know he only says it
because Mom's not around.

              "It's your boy." I hand him the phone and he
                    lightly shoves me in my shoulder.
It's *his* turn.

          "Hey, Dad, wassup?"
I watch him from the couch as he   gets on his
    serious look,
which is always the look   he has on when   talking to
    Dad.

He nods.

          "Yeah, yeah, I'm good. School, team
                workouts, same old thing."
He shakes his head.

          "Yeah, yeah, I know."
He exhales.

          "Umm, visit? Yeah, okay, sure."

I open my eyes a little wider as if that   can   make me
    hear the other end of

                                                X's call.

            "Yeah, call me and let me know if you can
                make it. It's okay if you can't. Okay, yeah,
                no problem. Later, Dad."
He ends the call and tosses me the phone.
I look up at him.
                "He says he's coming to see you?"
He just shakes his head and   walks away.
I guess Dad is
Xander's cavity

                                        too.

21. WHEN WE WERE YOUNGER

X and I were closer than Velcro
at least   that's what Mom says.
Especially after Dad left us   when I was in first
    grade   *I think*
and we lost our apartment
and had to stay at a shelter for *too long*.

He would keep us real busy
with fun activities.

       "Rain, what you wanna play?"
he would ask after pouring me out a bowl of cereal
from a box that would be halfway done
because
Xander ate *everything*.

I knew he would want to go play outside
even though I didn't want to.
       "Umm, I guess we can go outside."
He looked at me.
       "You sure?"
       "Yeah."
       "How about we play with your teddy bear
           first?"
My eyes would light up real big and bright.
       "Okay!"
And I'd eat my cereal so fast because *my* brother,
the kid that everyone waited at the park for,
wanted to play with me *first*.

22. IF ONLY

At   Hope Church
where I know Amare from,
I lean my head down on X's shoulder,
while the pastor preaches,
dozing in and out.

"Rain," he whispers. "If you fall asleep one more time,
    I'm telling Ma."
I can *hear* the smile in his voice.
I laugh real low.
Mom hates missing church
even for paying bills,
but sleeping in church is an even worse   no-no.
"Okay, okay, I'm sorry."
Music starts playing and I
open my eyes to see
these girls   and boys   in white and gold
moving   spinning   dancing
with flags
flags of all colors   mixing together   like a rainbow

in sync with the beat
slow together
then fast.
My eyes widen.
I smile
I clap

                and suddenly
                   my heart is still
                      from the beauty
                        of it all.

After church
the dance leader   Sade
who carries flags under her arms,
who I've known most of my life,
gives me a hug and says her usual
        "We still have a spot for you," and pokes me
              in my dimple.
Me? Have people looking at *me?*
I would love to dance and spin within the rainbow of colors.
But instead I say
        "We have to go catch the bus home, bye!"

23. XANDER AND I STAND AT THE BUS STOP

"Yo, Rain! Xander!"
We both look across the street from Hope Church
and see Amare waving us down
from his mom's car.
Xander links his arm with mine as we cross the busy,
    snowy street.
Mrs. Porter's minivan doors slide open.   X and I hop in.
"Thank you, Mrs. Porter," we both say.
She adjusts her rearview mirror and looks back at us.
"Anytime."
A rap song plays real low on the radio
so I know Amare's in charge of the music.
I stare out the foggy window   grateful for the
    warmth of the car.

Amare looks back at me.
"What's good, Rain?"
He reaches out his hand and daps me up.

"Amare, my guy." Xander daps him up.

"Rain, can you try to convince my mom to bake some
    mac and cheese for dinner tonight?"

I laugh.

Mrs. Porter is *known* for her mac and cheese at every
church function

school event

birthday party.

"Amare thinks I'm his personal chef." Mrs. Porter smiles
    through her rearview mirror.

"Why doesn't he ever offer to cook for *me*?"

"I don't want you getting sick though," I say.

"Really, Rain? You're really playing me?" Amare.

We all laugh.

"Oh yeah, Rain, are you coming tonight? To Dante's?"

Dante's?

"Dante's?"

"Yeah, for the movie night thing? Nara's going."

"Nara's going?"

"Of course. You're not?"

I feel Xander's body shift my way.

                          He looks at me

but I don't look back.

"I—uh—"

"Matter of fact, Mrs. Porter, can you drop us off right
    here?" Xander asks.

I look over at him, then outside at the grocery mart

that's close to where we live.

"You sure?" She looks at us again through
the rearview mirror.

The minivan doors open.

"Positive! Thank you again, Mrs. Porter!"

"Tell your mom I said hello!"

"Will do! Later, Amare!"

"Later, X! See you later, Rain?"

"Thank you, Mrs. Porter," I whisper. "Bye,
Amare."

I float my way into the grocery mart in disbelief at what
Amare said.

I feel that familiar pain in my chest.

"I'll get us some snacks," Xander says.

I nod.

The movie night thing.

Nara's going.

You're not?

24. LATER THAT NIGHT

I lie in bed
wondering
why I wasn't invited   by my own best friend
maybe because
of how I look   who I am
maybe I'm just   an embarrassment.

> *You're ugly.*
> *You're not good enough.*
> *You're worthless.*
> *Nobody likes you.*
> *Only bad things will happen.*

"What are you up to?" Xander knocks on my bedroom
     door.
"Noth . . . Nothing." I wipe away the tears from my face.
He walks in.
"What's that?" I point to a textbook in his hand.
He sits on the edge of my bed.

"This?" He holds it up. "A book on psychology. My
   favorite class."
"That's cool."
"You know what psychology is, don't you?" He smiles.
I push him in the shoulder.
"You think because I'm not at Elite Prep that I don't
   know?"
He frowns.
"No, no, I don't. I was kidding, Rain, I—"
"X, I'm kidding too, take it easy." I take the book from
   his hands. "Psychology, huh? Your favorite? I didn't
   know that. I thought math was your favorite, or . . .
   gym."
I flip through the pages.
"Don't get me wrong, I love math."
I scrunch my face at the thought.
"Love?"
"Yes, ma'am." He takes the book back. "But
   psychology—how the mind works, how people
   think—it's pretty dope. I'm obsessed with this stuff."
"That's not so bad, I guess." I shrug.

He stands up.
"All right, Rain-drop, I'm going to study for this test.
   You get some rest."

"Okay," I whisper.

He leaves   and
                   I try to fight it   but

                                        the tears are back.

25. WHILE WALKING DOWN THE HALLWAY AT SCHOOL

I see a flyer taped to the wall for a step team.   I stop
     at it.
Step? Here?
"Nara, look!" I smile wide.
I point at it for her to see.
She looks back and laughs.
"*You*, Rain, really?"
Huh?
"We did it in elementary school, remember? We used to
     have so much fun. Do you remember that one step
     we did for the Christmas program?"

I start clapping and stomping from muscle memory.

I can't believe I still remember it.

                            It was so much fun.

She looks down at her phone.

"Yeah, we did everything together, but that's wack.
     You'd really do that, *now?*"

"Umm . . . no . . . I just thought . . . I thought you'd want
     to . . . and if you did it . . . I'd do it too."

"Yeah, nah."

She walks off.

I look at the flyer one more time and walk off too.

          "Okay."

26. FANTASTIC FOUR

Andre aka Dre Dre
Julanie aka Jay, and
Nicholas aka Butter   *because his game's smooth*
are over as usual.
When they're over
they're watching and talking
football, basketball, and girls.
Lately I've been noticing that
            I look nothing like these girls on their phones.

Like X,   these guys all big and tall
and have basically been my brothers since
X was in elementary school.

I watch them from the kitchen table as I
try to do my math homework.
Dre Dre jumps up.
"Yo, X, when you leaving bougie-ass Elite Prep to come
      ball with *us* at City High?"

I roll my eyes.

X walks over to them with a big bag of chips.

"Nah, nah, chill. Y'all know I love my city, but Elite's
    where it's at when it comes to scouting."

Dre Dre waves him off like what he just said was
    nonsense.

"Don't *hate,* Dre!" Jay grabs the chips from X.

"X finna make it to the big league and you out here
    crying for him to come play with us!"

They all laugh.

                                        I laugh too.

"Nah, it'd be dope with *all* of us on a team. Remember
    those days? Yo, there was no stopping us, no way."
    Xander.

"You right, man. Fantastic Four all the way, man." Jay.

"No doubt." Butter.

X walks over to the kitchen to get juice and

plucks me in the head   *just because.*

I hit his arm.

        "Go away."

He walks back out into the living room.

            "Y'all know I'm going on a college visit to
                Smith University next week, right?"

He sits down on the sofa.

   "Oh man, here we go, more of the Elite,"
   Butter says.

We all know what he means.
More people who don't look like Xander.

   "Don't hate." Jay shakes his head.
   "Who you goin' with?" Butter. "That Zach
   dude, right? Gotta be. You ain't got no
   Black friends at your school?"

Whoa.
X laughs.

   "*Chill*, Butter, you wildin'. Zach's mad cool."
Dre Dre nods.

   "Zach's pretty dope."
Butter shakes his head.

   "Yeah, y'all go ahead and keep thinking that
   they're on our side."
X looks back at me and I raise my eyebrows
  knowing exactly why he thinks *they* wouldn't be.

27. A CONTAINER OF MIRACLE

Mom gets a day off and makes me go to the grocery
   store with her
         in the busiest part of the City
               and I hate it.
I hate holding bags.
I hate food shopping during the beginning of the
   month when
everybody goes food shopping.

When we're a block away from the grocery store
       plastic bags hurting my wrists
       the cold wind   in my face
Mom wants to stop at the beauty supply store.
      "For some hair product for *us*." She smiles
and pinches my cheek but I
roll my eyes because   she knows   how much
   I get frustrated with   my hair.

We walk into the hair store
owned by people who don't look like   us.

We get eyed at
because we're carrying bags
as if we're going to steal something
                    but Mom pays them no mind.

I walk around
then get stuck looking at different-colored lipsticks and
I don't see where Mom goes.
I keep walking and end up
in an unfamiliar aisle
stocked with products that say:
                    Lightening Cream
                    Skin Bleaching Crème
                    Whitening Cream

On them are faces of
light-skinned women
whose skin went from black to light,
black to white,
dark to pale.
          My heart stops at how nice and clear their
                skin looks.
          I take up a container of miracle.
I need this.

"Rain!"
I jump,

dropping the product.
I pick it up
and put it back on the shelf.
"Coming, Mommy!"

28. NARA'S OVER

And although it seems like the right time
to bring up the movie night that Amare mentioned,
I don't.
I'm just glad she's here.
She walks into my crowded little room.

      "My mom got me this shirt." I tug on the tee
         I have on.
The one I purposely put on knowing she'd be coming
   over.

      "Girl, you look fine," she says, but she's not
        actually *looking* at me when she says it.
She sits on my bed.
She lifts up my teddy bear.
      "I can't believe you still have this."
I notice how skinny she looks.

A little knot forms in my stomach.

                "Yeah, I mean, it was a gift—"

Her phone alerts and she looks at it   smiling   but
    doesn't show me.

I'm hungry but don't say it.

That night   after Nara's dad picks her up
I write in the orange journal from Miss Walia:

> I'm so glad that Nara came over today.
> I'm so happy that she's my friend.
> My closest friend since we were little.
> And as we get older, although I'm not as
> popular as she is, she's still here.
> That's real friendship.

I close the journal and press it against my
    chest   *so happy* to have Nara
                      in my life   still.

29. LITTLE DAD

Mom always says that
when I was real young I
would grab Xander's legs and scream
in public
         "This is my little dad!"

When Mom couldn't make it
to parent-teacher conferences
it was X who would show up   in one of his church
   suits
me in second grade   him in sixth,
sitting in front of my teacher saying,
        "I'm here in place of my mom."

And since everybody loved X   they let him do it,
and in more ways than one
X is *still* my little dad.
        "Did you eat?"
Xander walks up to the kitchen table with his gym bag.
        "Yeah," I lie,

looking down at the jiggle of my thighs.
I don't deserve to eat.
I have enough fat on my body to last me a lifetime.
        With him being home late from weight-
           room workouts at school and
        Mommy working the overnight shift
            again   he didn't know if I had.
He eyes me suspiciously.
        "Aiight, Rain-drop. Need any help with
           homework?"
He sits down in front of me obviously tired,
but willing.
        "You know I need your super math strength,
           X-Man."
He laughs.
So do I.
        I love my brother
        even though sometimes I pretend like I don't.

No one can distract me from my sadness like he can.

30. HAIR LIKE HERS

At Nara's house we're watching music videos in her
    room,
when out of nowhere she touches my hair and says,
        "Rain, why don't you do something with
                your *hair*?"
I shrug and say,
        "I dunno,"
even though I cried this morning after sneaking Mom's
straightening iron into the bathroom
to try to get my hair like hers.
I quickly wipe a tear from my eye when she's not
    looking.
I know she doesn't mean it
but sometimes her words come with
sharp edges.

31. XANDER IS INSTRUCTED BY MOM

To brush my hair
that breaks combs,
that hurts when pulled,
that's too thick for Xander's grasp.

His football hands
cannot catch,
tackle,
defend himself,
while he brushes.
      "Ouch!"
I flinch,
reach for my
screaming scalp.
      "My bad,"
he breathes,
frustrated,
standing like Mom does
when she does
my hair.

I've gotten too tall
to sit on the sofa,
me in between her strong calves
her legs soft as shea butter.

             "I'm done."
Xander hands me the brush,
wipes his forehead with the
back of his wrist, and
walks away
because no one can do

what Mom does.

32. XANDER IS BACK

To studying when Mom walks in from work.

> "Thank you, Xander." She kisses him on the
> cheek.
>
> "Hi, Mommy."
>
> "I got this for you." She hands me a pack of
> beads, then sits around the kitchen table
> with us.
>
> "Beads?"

I smile.

It's been a long time since Mom put beads in my hair.

I hug her.

> "Nice, right? Look at the patterns, the
> different browns."

I nod.

> "Thank you, Mommy."

She pinches my cheek.

I wonder if Nara will like these beads.

> "Well, I'm off to take a shower. Today was
> exhausting!"

Ma stands up, cries out, holding the lower part of her
    back.
            "Ma!" Xander stands up and holds her.
She laughs.
            "I think I might've pulled something today.
                Don't worry about me."
            "Ma—"
            "Just worry about your workouts."
Xander looks down at me.
I shrug.
            "Okay," he whispers.

33. WHEN WE WERE YOUNGER

Sometimes *Dad* would pick Xander up
and take him to the park without me.
"I'll be right back, okay?" X would squeeze me
            pressing
his football and basketball   against my shoulders.
"Okay," I'd whisper with tears in my eyes.

And then he'd go and I'd go   find Mom.

"Mommy . . ." I'd push open the bedroom door and
      she'd be sleeping   tired
from everything moms do   and I'd
tiptoe back out   imagining   pretending
I was a bunny   hopping slightly.
I'd go find paper   a pen   scissors
to make a card for Xander   since I was feeling sad.
I'd sit on the living room floor   cutting the paper
      into the shape of a heart,
reading it aloud as I wrote,
"Dear Xander, thank you for being the funnest and
      coolest big brother ever. Love you more than ice
      cream with cherries, sprinkles, and chocolate syrup.
      Love, Rain."
Then I'd sit and wait   with Mr. Snuggles
reading the card   over and over   a million
      times.

When Xander came home,
it seemed darker than when he'd usually come home.
I expected Dad to come inside with him.   But he
      didn't.   Not even to say hello.
I looked up at X's sweaty face,   which looked
      worried,
his shirt extra dirty.

"Xander, what happened?"

"Nothing, nothing!"

He dropped the football and basketball to the ground
and squeezed me and slightly lifted me in the air.

I squealed for joy.

"Where's Dad?" I asked.

Xander looked back at the door.

"He's . . . He had some work stuff."

Then a thought came to my head,

that maybe if I would've made Dad a card too   he
        would've come inside to see me.

"What's this?" Xander walked over to the floor where
        his card was.

"I made it for you!"

"Rain-drop, this is dope, I love it. . . . Where's Ma?"

I pointed in the direction of the room.

"Sleeping?" he asked, with a small frown.

"Yup." I smiled, still ecstatic about the card,
            but then I remembered Dad. "How was
            the park?"

"It was . . . It was aiight."

34. IT ALL DEPENDS

"Miss Washington!"
I turn around and it's Mr. Jackson
walking down   the hall   toward me.
Vice principal of City Middle School
football coach   and
Xander's #1 fan.

"How are you, Rain?"
I shrug because
I'm late for class.
"I'm good."
I know what's coming.
"And how's Xander?"
"He's good."
"I'm glad! Tell him I said hello! I'm so glad he got out
      before it was too late."

People always say that about the young men
in my City

that it gets   *too late*   for them after a certain point.
But I say
it all
depends.

      Depends on what you got
      who you got   and most importantly

                who's got you.

35. IN MISS WALIA'S CLASS

I'm thinking about X leaving for his college visit.
My heart is beating   hard
in my chest.
I look over at Nara, who's half writing,
half typing in her cell phone that's hiding in her
    lap,   hoping
she'll notice.
Some sort of   *best friend connection*   or something.

I take the orange journal out of my book bag
and write:

I don't want X to leave.

"Glad you're using your journal, Rain."

I jump.

Miss Walia is standing in front of my desk.

"Oh!" I look up at her. I smile. "Thank you."

I write:

Miss Walia made me smile today.

36. DESERVE

I help Xander pack for his trip to Smith University
as he talks real loud on the phone with Zach.
"Bro, it's gonna be *lit!*"
Lit?

A college visit?
I roll my eyes and stuff more socks into one of his
    duffel bags.
"Loser," I mouth to him,
and he throws one of his pillows at me.
I dodge it and laugh,
        stick my tongue out.

He mouths, "You just wait."
I'm really going to miss my brother.

Especially when the sadness

hits.

But Zach's parents are already outside
to take him and X
to Elite Prep to get on the bus for their *fancy college trip.*
X is finally all packed
and has said a thousand goodbyes.

But before he can get out the front door,
Mom stands in front of him   on her toes,
and holds his face the way
someone holds up the body of a newborn.
Like a cradle,
like something fragile,
in awe
in love
in admiration, and says,
"You, Xander, deserve to be there."

37. I CALL X

"Hello? X?"

"Rain." He yawns.
"Yeah."
"Wassup? You aiight?"
"Yeah, you reached yet?"
"Nah, not yet." He yawns again.
"Oh, okay. Just calling."
He laughs.
"Miss you too, Rain. You'll be aiight."
"I know."
"Love you, sis, good night."
"Night, X, love you."

38. FILTER

I sleep over at Nara's house for the weekend
since Xander's gone on his trip,
but Nara's planning on ditching me for *Dante*.

She takes mirror pictures after throwing on a sweater
    and some jeans
and looks pretty so easily,
and I think about how I *never ever*
like any of the pictures I'm in.
                          Nara never needs a filter.
I look over at a picture of us in first grade that's in a
    frame on her dresser.
        "See you later, Rain."
        "Bye, Na—"
and she's out.

So I just   wait,
looking around her room   full of mirrors   and
    girl things
meant for the skinny and the pretty.

My room looks more like storage for me and Mom's
    things.

Mom   who   lets me sleep on the bed
while she
sleeps on the sofa.

I look out the window and see it's getting late,

wondering what Nara and Dante are doing and
wondering when Mr. or Mrs. Jones will take me home.

But instead Mrs. Jones walks into Nara's room
looking all flustered and says,
            "R-Rain, your mom, your mom needs you to
            stay an extra night here."
            "Why? What happened?"
Mom's never *needed* me to stay an extra night here
    before.
She looks me in the eyes
silent for a second,
then says,
            "Rain, something happened to Xander on his
            trip."

My eyes widen and I repeat in my head
a sentence I've *never* heard before in my life:

Something happened to Xander.
Something happened to Xander.
Something happened to Xander.

She walks out.

I lie down
but I don't sleep.
What does that mean?
The way she said it and
the way she looked   scares me.
I put my hand over my mouth
to stop myself
from vomiting out
the sick feeling in my stomach.

39. I TEXT XANDER

X doesn't text me back.
      I text him almost a thousand emojis,

          and the funniest GIFs I can find.
But nothing
      no comeback emoji
         no *LOL*

            no *Shuddup Rain-drop.*
I'm feeling uneasy because Xander always
writes me back.
      I can't sleep. I can't sleep. I can't sleep.
Why isn't anyone

      telling me

        anything?

40. MOM CALLS

Early
the next
morning—
>"*Mommy?*"
>"Hey, baby, how are you?"
>"Mommy, whereareyouandwhycan'tIcome
>>homeandwhathappenedtoXander?"

The phone grows quiet.
>"*Mommy?*"
>"Baby, Xander . . . Xander got hurt."

Hurt?
>"Hurt? How'd he get hurt? Was he working
>>out or something?"

I can hear a lot of noise in her background.
>"They're saying it was . . . Wait . . . Baby, let
>>me call you back. I love you, okay, baby?
>>Mommy loves you."
>"Love you too, but Mommy . . ."

I look down at the phone and
she's gone.

Nara watches me as I sit on her bed
legs crossed
watching the phone in my hand   waiting for Mom to
                                    call me back

                                but she doesn't.

41. I DON'T WAIT

Mrs. Jones is driving me home   *finally.*
But I can't help but think about
          Mom's voice over the phone,
how it didn't sound like her.
I look out the window at the other cars,
the trees,
            the people,
                    everything just seems so
                                                still.
My heart and mind race.
                    How could X get hurt on his trip?
                    Was he playing around?

Is he sick?
But sick isn't hurt,   or is it?

I've never seen X get hurt really bad,
a sprain or two   but   he barely even gets a cold
    anymore.
            "How are you feeling, Rain?"
It's a red light so she looks my way,
but I refuse to make eye contact.

Mrs. Jones plays with the radio but
doesn't turn it on.

        "I'm good," I lie.
I dust my jeans to calm my nerves,
but I can't help but   *feel like throwing up.*

        "Rain," she breathes.
I look up from my jeans to see
three cop cars parked outside my home.
I don't wait for the car to fully stop to
run
run
run

out.

42. I RUN

Across the street   up the steps   into our
     apartment
my heart
beating like a drum   my eyes widening like satellites.
I see officers standing in my living room

                                                  nothing feels real
Why are they here?
Where's Xander?!
          "Mommy!" I scream.
She runs out from the kitchen and
grabs my hands.
          "M-M-Mommy, what's g-g-going on?"
"Rain." Her voice cracks.
She exhales, but it's a   painful groan that makes
tears well in my eyes.
"Rain . . . Xander's in the hospital."
What did she just say? Hospital? Xander's in the hospital?
"W-w-w-what?"
Mom keeps talking   hand against her forehead.

"At some college party, Rain. They beat Xander up. . . .

It's . . . it's bad. . . . It's *real* bad."

I look into the red of her eyes, wet with tears.

My legs become Jell-O.

"Why?"

43. BREAK

Mom and I   are on a train   to go meet X,
in the city   where he   took his trip.

Mommy wipes my tears as her own face is flooding.

We're met by a police escort at the hospital,
and follow them to the unit that Xander's in.
I take off running down shiny white halls
that smell like *broken things* as if
I could detect my brother without guidance   as if
I was given
directions.

Running
as if I know what I'm doing,
running
as if this whole thing is a dream,
tears
running
down my face.

Xander, where are you?

"Rain!"

Please let me find you!

I look back and Mom stands with the officers at a
    doorway.

She presses a tissue to her face as I walk over.
            "Rain, please just—"

I walk into the room to see Xander lying on a bed.

His face
swollen   *so swollen*
bruised and bloodied.

Oh my God.

I hold my face in my hands.

I've never seen someone hurt like this. Especially not
    my brother. Not Xander.

I walk up to him and his eyes meet mine.

        "Xander."

I touch his shoulder and Mom

                holds
                me as
                I
                b r e a k.

44. LIKE THIS

Mom walks over with the suited men, with more
    tissues in her hand.
I can barely look up.
        "Rain, this is Detective Foster and Detective
            Kelly."
I nod as chills run through my body.
        They stretch out their hands for me to
            shake,
but my hands are sweaty and limp,
so I hold my knees instead.
        "Hello, Rain. Detective Foster and I are here
            to help your family find out who the—"
        "Eighteen-year-old high school seniors from
            Elite Preparatory Academy Zachary Taylor
            and Xander Washington were on a college
            visit to Smith University when they were
            beaten relentlessly at a college party . . ."

I look at the hanging television above the detectives'
    heads.

"Video has been released of the brawl . . ."
I cover my mouth as a blurry
cell phone video
plays of
people stomping
            kicking
                    punching
                            my seemingly
                    motionless brother on the ground.
Mom starts screaming.
            I put my hands over my ears,   terrified.
She punches her fists into the chest of the detective.
One of the officers rushes over to restrain her.
A nurse is calling out,
            "Ma'am, ma'am!"
I'm screaming
            "Mommy!"
because I've never seen Mom this way   before.

Mom cries out,
            "My baby, my baby! Why are they showing
                my baby *like this*?"

45. DISAPPEAR

Mom is sleeping next to me in my bed tonight.
I can't stop shaking,   I can't stop seeing Xander's
    face.
I can't stop hurting for him   on the inside.
My sadness is swallowing me up whole,
even with Mom next to me.
She can't stop it.
No one can stop this.

Mom's arms wrap around my body
like a quilt of warm skin.
She rocks me and
hums a song from church.
I can't help but wonder why God would let this happen
    to Xander.

"He'll be home soon," she whispers gently.
Although when we got home from the hospital
I heard how she cried,
        how she prayed so hard

it shook my bones.
How she clapped her hands,
how she stomped her feet
in frustration,
how I held myself so tight
praying that I might
disappear.

46. WHEN WE WERE YOUNGER

Xander would take me to the park during the
summertime.
Mom didn't work as much then.
Instead
she would sleep.
And Mom slept a lot at the shelter.

So Xander would be the one to take me out.

"We're going to the park," Xander would say.
"But I ain't got nothing to wear," I'd complain.

"You mean, you don't *have anything* to wear," he'd
     correct me.
He'd give me one of his T-shirts, which would go
all the way down to my knees.
"See how fly you look, Rain-drop? You're as fly as me
     now."
He'd smile wide and I'd believe him,
twirling around in that shirt like Cinderella owned it
     before me.
We'd walk to the park in the heat
and Xander would let me play on the jungle gym,
while he played on the ball court.

"Drink some water, Rain!"
he would scream out while dribbling or making a shot
and everybody would just look at me
as I walked to the water fountain.

It was then that I would notice
that I was the only little girl
wearing her big brother's oversized T-shirt.
So I tried to keep to myself at the park
although I'd watch and smile
at the fun other kids were having
from my swing,   my safe place.
I could push myself real high on my own.

"Rain!"
Xander was walking over to me and I realized that
he was wearing the same thing he wore to the park
the last time we came,
and the time before that, too.
But Xander's game was *so* nice
that I don't think anybody noticed.

He came close and pushed me on the swing so high
that
I swore I was going to touch the sky,
and I laughed so hard that tears started falling from my
eyes.
I could push myself even higher with my brother's help.

Then kids would start running out of nowhere,
and we'd both see the ice cream truck pull up.
"You want something, Rain?"
He pulled some coins out his pocket.
He never waited for me to answer.
"I'll be back."
And I would see kids come back from the truck
with ice cream cones with sprinkles,
frozen cartoon characters with gumballs for eyes.
Icees in rainbow colors.
Then X would come back with a fifty-cent bag of chips,
take out about four chips, and say,

"Here, the rest is yours."
I'd take the bag and look up at him.
"You sure?"
"Of course." He'd start running back to the ball court.
"And don't forget to drink water!"

47. MEMORY

Mom has to miss a whole lot of work
to visit Xander during the day
and sleep next to me during the night.
Because I can't sleep alone anymore.
Because I'm afraid.

Although Mom allows me to stay home from school
I don't go with her to see him.   I can't.
Even when I try,   I can't.
If I stand to go,   I can't move.
My legs won't move. So I sit back down.
And try not to think of how broken he looked.
How much he *didn't* look like Xander.

But it's hard.
Because God gave us memory
of even the things we don't want to remember.

48. INNOCENT

I sit in front
of the television, which
Mom has turned on while she paces the house,
on the telephone with *this person* and *that person*.

Xander is all over the news and we
just can't escape it.
The video has gone viral.
And now I know why they use the term *viral* for *diseases*
                              because I'm feeling so *sick*.
The news calls Xander a victim
a target.
Not Xceptional,
not Xcellent,
they mention that he's *Black* twenty times,

as if it's hard to see,   *as if we don't know what*
        Black skin looks like.

But what
they don't call him is
innocent.

49. EVERY DAY I SPEND HOURS

On the bathroom floor.
Knees hard against the cold tiles.

I hold my stomach.
And cry out.

Sometimes the cry is quiet.
Sometimes it's *so* loud that I have to check if Mom is
        walking in.

One moment I'm crying for X.
The next moment I'm lost in my own sadness.

You're ugly.
You're not good enough.
You're worthless.
Nobody likes you.
Only bad things will happen.
And then it all just mixes together like paint.
Like clouds.
Like a tornado.

Is this how other kids feel when they're sad?
What do kids do in the movies? In the shows?
On social media?

Does anybody   *ever hurt*   *the way I hurt?*
Does anybody   *ever hurt*   *like me?*

50. MOM EXPLAINS

I sit at the kitchen table and try to eat cereal
that has become soggy and cold.

I can hear every word
the detective has to say through Mom's phone.
Words like
battery
assault
which make me swallow hard.
Tears salt my milk because
I don't want Xander in the hospital.
I want him here with us.

Mom ends the call and turns her head in the direction
    of the living room.
The TV's on.
It's muted but there it is again,
Xander's incident   on the news.
I forgot to turn it off before she could see it.

I don't tell her that I'm constantly watching   and
      scrolling
to hear what the world is saying about my brother.
      My brother.
It seems like the world knows more about him than I
      do right now.
It seems like I'm losing him to everybody else
      right now.
I don't tell her that I feel exposed,
even from within our home.
She exhales deeply,
her eyes more sunken than ever before.

"Why do they keep putting that video up? He's just a
      baby."
I know it's not *me* she's talking to,   but society.
Her frustration causes a sharp pain in my back. What I
      want to say,
I try not to say.
But I have to say it.
"What . . . happened?"

Her eyes let me know that she knows what I really
      mean.
Why did it happen to Xander?
Who did it?
Why would they do it?

What happened to Zach?

She exhales again and immediately I feel terrible for
asking.

"From what Zach said . . ."

"Was Zach put in the hospital?"

"He wasn't admitted."

"Was he hurt?"

"He had a couple of bruises."

"A *couple?*"

She nods.

"According to Zach, they went to this frat party. A lot
of people were drinking. Some people were messing
with them. Some girls from a sorority were dancing
with them and some people weren't happy about
that," Mom explains.

Wait—what?

"And they . . . *jumped* him for that?"

"Zach said someone hit him and Xander stood up for
him. And then he got jumped."

"Why would Zach leave him, though? I barely saw him
in the video." Tears fill my eyes.

"He said he had to get help."

Is she defending him?

"But *Xander* needed help."

I'm hurt thinking of Zach abandoning Xander like that.

51. SELFISH

I run to the bathroom anytime the doorbell rings.
I don't want to be here.   *I can't be here.*   *I*
     can't live like this.
My heart beats fast.   I lock the door.   I sit on the
     toilet.
I'm tired of detectives and lawyers,
newspapers.
I call them all dragons,   breathing fire.
Leaving behind smoke that nobody can see through.
     I think they call this hyperventilating.
I run the bathwater to drown out their voices.
I can't live like this.
I miss Xander so much—
     he would've protected me from all of this.
But no one can protect me,

and who's protecting him?

Mom says we have to
     keep praying and
     remain hopeful but

it's too hard right now.
And because I don't want to come with her
to the hospital, she said she'd call me
to speak to Xander.
That he's doing *better.*
I pace our home all day.

I lie in Xander's bed to try to remember him in the right
     way,
to form the right words,
to have the right mood   despite his current
     condition.
My phone vibrates and my heart pounds.
I almost run to the bathroom but instead I answer the
     call,
squeezing Xander's pillow tight to my chest.
          "He-hello?"
          "Rain!" It's Mom. "Say hi to Xander. He can
              hear you!"
I'm on speaker.
          "Hi, Xander!" I switch to casual. "Hey, X!"
          "Hey."
I can barely hear him.
          "How are you? You okay?"
          "He's doing much better!" Mom's voice is *way*
              too happy.
          "Okay, that's good," I mumble.

Doesn't he want to know if *I'm* okay?
Is that selfish of me?
          "I'll be home soon, Rain! Will call you back!
                    Love you!"
          "Oh, okay. Love you too."

52. I KNOW WHAT MOM IS GOING TO ASK

Before she asks it.
          "Do you want to come today?"
She's getting dressed,   which
now involves a lot of pacing and phone calls.
          "No."
It's snowing a lot today and the snowstorm outside
feels like it's also inside me.
I go into my room and find the orange journal from
    Miss Walia,
tear out a page, and write:
    Hi X,
    Mommy says you'll be home soon, and I can't wait!

Have you thought of any crazy things to cook?
I miss your cooking but mostly you.
Please don't worry too much.
I love you!

I fold it up and only hand it to her
after her goodbye and kisses.
When she closes the front door,
I am alone   with my thoughts   again.

53. WHEN WE WERE YOUNGER

When Xander was in elementary school,
occasionally he would get headaches   *bad* headaches.
          "*Mommy,*" he'd cry.
I'd trail behind Mom as she made him peppermint tea,
place a warm rag on his forehead,
and give him some medicine.
And then I'd feel it.
A *headache.*
Watching *him* gave *me* a *headache.*
And Mom would make *me* peppermint tea,

place a warm rag on *my* forehead,
and give *me* some medicine.
We'd both lie in the bed we shared   and
I wouldn't get better until he did.

54. WHEN WE WERE YOUNGER

And I was at one of Xander's home football games with
    City Middle School,
he sprained his ankle right on the field.
Right there   in front of me   in front of everyone.
He got tackled by someone on the other team and fell
and cried out in pain.

And I ran.

I ran so fast   to the field.
Before the trainer,
the medic,
the coach.
The referees' whistles
        sounded like a soundtrack to my own horror film.

I was crying once I got to him and
Xander looked up at me and said,
"Rain, I'm good, I promise."

55. I HEAR FOOTSTEPS BUT I CAN'T MOVE

"Rain?" It's Mom.
I am startled out of memory.
I am on my bed   cocooned in blankets.
I can't open my mouth to speak.
No, I'm not asleep.
Yes, I hear you.
No, I'm not okay.
*Yes, I know Xander is alive and well, but something is dead
    inside me.*

"Good night, baby." The door closes.

56. I FINALLY SPEAK TO DAD

Although he's been speaking to Mom every day.
The most   he's ever called.
The most   he's ever asked about Xander and
ugh   *Ray Ray.*
"How've you been holding up?"
His words feel bland,   like oatmeal made with
   water and nothing else.
Mom sits down on my bed next to me to ensure that I
   actually respond.
"I . . ." I look down. "I'm okay."
He goes on,
"That's good to hear, Ray Ray. This whole thing has
   been insane."
I don't understand how this affects him.
I stay silent for a while until Mom looks at me with
   wide, concerned eyes.
I find a safe answer.
       "It has been."

When Mom is back at the hospital,
she makes me speak to Xander again.
And like the last time   he's barely speaking.
And although I know he's in *new* pain, I'm expecting
    the *old* him.
"How are you?" I ask.
"Okay." His voice like cotton.
"I miss you so much, but I know you're coming home
    soon."
He exhales sharply.
"Miss you too."
And I'm missing the *Rain-drop.*
I'm missing my Xander.

After we hang up
I try to pray   like Mom says   but it's hard.
Where do I even start?
So instead, I take out the orange journal from Miss
    Walia and write:

> Mommy says to pray, but it's too hard. It's too
> hard to try to pray right now. It's easier to write
> my words, but even writing is becoming harder
> because of how sad I feel. Life doesn't feel too
> good right now and there's no way that I can
> fix it. Even Mommy can't fix it. God, why do we
> have to go through this? We didn't deserve this.

X didn't deserve this. Why can't things just go
back to the way they were? Can't You just fix it
already?

57. NOT SO FANTASTIC

Andre aka Dre Dre,
Julanie aka Jay,
and Nicholas aka Butter

cause his game's smooth
are over and it's *not* usual.
I watch them from the kitchen
because I'm scared.
Today is the first day that
it doesn't feel good to have them here   without X.

Mom lets them know
that the detectives want to ask them questions   to
    know more about Xander prior to the incident.
"This don't make no sense!"
Butter is pacing back and forth in the living room.

Dre Dre and Jay are sitting on the arms of the sofa.

    Mom's standing against the wall next to them.

Looking at me,   looking at them.

I'm struggling to breathe.

"Take it easy, man." Dre Dre.

"Yeah, come on, man. Chill out." Jay.

"Maybe you guys *should* talk to them," Mom says. "I'll

    be there, and a lawyer will be present."

I look over at Mom

who sounds   unconvinced by her own words.

        "Talk to them about what exactly, Ma?"

                Butter. "About the fact that my friend
                was the only Black person on that trip
                and he's the one to end up battered at
                some stupid-ass, wack-ass frat party?
                What they want me to say? Huh? That
                X is some hoodlum? That he's a football
                player so he's aggressive? Tell them
                that he started it, Ma? Caused his own
                pain? That his bozo white friend is the
                innocent one? What they want me to
                say?"

        "Yo, Butter. Breathe, man." Dre Dre stands
                up.

        "*Breathe?* X could've gotten killed! They
                had to *carry* him out—you ain't seen the
                video, Dre? You ain't seen our boy bloody

with a whole concussion? What he had,
Ma—broken ribs, right?"
Jay looks away.
"I ain't got nothing to say. Why it had to be
X, huh? X—who out of all us is always
doing the right thing? He could've died—
don't you see that? My boy couldn't
even open his eyes! What kind of
confrontation is that? That ain't fair! He
could've *died*!"
Butter covers his face with his hands and starts crying.
And then we're all crying,
because the Fantastic Four is
not so fantastic right now.

I could form a lake with all the tears this has caused,
a permanent lump has formed in my throat,
and my body has chills running through it,
so many chills.
"I'll talk to them," Butter says through tears.
"For X."

58. WHEN WE WERE YOUNGER

I would watch Xander, Dre Dre, Jay, and Butter
play football in the street
in good and bad weather.
They'd have me be the lookout for incoming cars
although they'd rarely hit any,
but it still made me feel important.

I was everywhere they were,
at every practice   for every sport,
because I couldn't be left at home alone.
So I'd sit   on some bench   in some gym,
and watch them   and feel safe   somehow,
and not as sad   as I usually would.
Coach Jackson   the vice principal at City Middle
    School
would give us a ride back
to the shelter.
"One day," Dre Dre would call out with a football in his
    hand,

leaned up against a parked car, "we're gonna make it to
    the big league."
Butter would catch next   then X   then Jay.
They would always compete to see who was the
    biggest
    fastest
    strongest
    smartest.
"Can't wait until we all get to City High and show them
    what the Fantastic Four is all about!" Butter would
    say.
They'd all agree   and cheer,   dap each other up,
but Xander would always look my way   with a small
    frown,
because he knew that I knew   that Mom
didn't want him going to no   City High.

59. MRS. PORTER IS COMING OVER

To drop off some food and I'm praying
praying *hard*   that she left Amare at home or
anywhere   but here.
I stay in my room,
hearing voices out there,
preparing to fake sleep.
"Rain?" A small knock.
Amare.
Sigh.

"Yeah?" I sit up, feeling as ridiculous as I probably look.
Amare walks in and just looks at me   silent.
In a way, he's like an unofficial cousin,
knowing him and his parents since I was real little at
     Hope Church.
His parents even helped us move here   after living
     in the shelter.
I'm not as embarrassed as I could be   as *I think I
     should be*

with Amare   seeing me
like this.

"Rain, you okay?"
Can he see them?
The dark clouds around me?
"Yeah, I'm tired and my head is hurting."
He nods.
I lie back down.
"Yeah, your mom said that. Okay, well, let me not
       interrupt your sleep. My mom and I brought some
       stuff for you guys."
"Thank you," I say, louder to my pillow than to Amare.
"And I also brought these," he says.
Brought what?
I look up to see him waving a pack of Uno cards.
I smile a little.
"*Really*, Amare?"
He raises his eyebrows at me.
Should I?
I exhale.
"Fine, fine." I pat the edge of my bed.
He sits down.
I sit up.
He shuffles the cards.
"What are the rules?" I ask as he hands me seven cards.
       "Or are you still cheating like you used to?"

He laughs, putting seven cards down for himself.

"Colors and numbers?" he asks.

I nod.

"Plus twos on plus fours?" he asks.

"*Never.* Twos with twos and fours with fours." I organize
  my cards.

"That's *boring.*"

He flips over the first card   a green three.

"You go," he says.

                    Green five.

Red five.

                    Red two.

Yellow two.

"You sure you're okay, Rain?" he asks.

I look up at him.

"To be honest, I'm not sure."

                    Plus four.

                    "Now pick up four cards." I smile.

60. ELITE PREPARATORY ACADEMY

Mom and I walk into X's
    private school
and I feel like a chocolate chip
drowning
in milk.

Eyes follow Mommy, Principal McGregor,
Detective Foster, and me.
I'm finally aware that skin is the
largest organ of the body.
I'm aware
how my hair
defies
gravity.
I fold in my lips
and walk real slow
down
perfect halls and perfect floors
that show my reflection.
It makes me start to   *pray myself invisible.*

Principal McGregor leads us into his office.
"Here we are. The Oval Office." He smiles.
A joke? Mom smiles shyly.
I barely look his way but sit on one of
the fancy maroon sofas,
which looks softer than it feels.
He sits at his big brown desk and Mom sits in front of
    him.
"Mrs. Washington, I can't imagine what you and your
    family are going through right now."
Mom nods.

The door opens and I look over to see Zach,
and his parents,
and Detective Kelly.
Zach looks straight at me
and I notice a black shadow around one of his eyes,
    not as bad as Xander's
but it's there.
But it doesn't matter   because he still betrayed X
so I ignore him the whole time.

That night Mom tells me
I'll have to go back to school soon,
although I don't want to.
        "I have to figure this out, Rain."
I'm not sure if she's trying to convince me   or herself.

61. FOR LATER

"Everybody's talking about Xander at school."
Nara's over and I'm feeling sick to my stomach.
She came right after I had another dry phone
     conversation with X   who Mom said
was in a lot of pain.
        "Oh." I lie in bed,
happy for the company
but somehow sad that she's here.
       "Yup."

She walks around my room,   with her cell phone
     in her hand.
"He's everywhere, on every website, *everything*. Are you
     getting all the links I've been sending you, girl?"
I nod my head yes, although I'm lying.
I barely look at my phone nowadays.
The world's access to my brother

                        hurts me.
But I bottle my tears for later,
my tongue feeling as dry as a desert.

I close my eyes, hoping   that
my sadness doesn't drown me,
imagining Xander standing by my side.

62. WHEN WE WERE YOUNGER

Mommy would let me go over to Nara's house to play.
One of her parents would pick me up,
and Nara would come with them.
I was always shocked when it was Mr. Jones.
Nara's dad was like a figment of my imagination,
because my dad was such a distant memory.

I would watch them in the car talking,
wondering what my dad could ever have to say to me.
"It's nice to see you, Rain." Mr. Jones would high-five
     me,
then ask how Mom and Xander were doing.
Although for some reason
I'd feel discomfort,
because the only guy I'd ever talk to was Xander
or my male teachers   *sometimes.*

Nara and I would play with all her dolls,
and she would *always* take charge.
At home,
Mommy would give me dozens of magazines she'd get
    from work
after cleaning people's houses
and I would cut out
people's faces   and furniture   and cars   and
    clothes
and give them names and move them around   and
    do different voices
and pretend they were real.
Xander would help me cut them out
and one time
I put them all carefully in a plastic bag,
            and brought them to Nara's house.
                    She saw them and she laughed *so* hard
            at me   at them   at my cutouts.
So I said,
        "I gotta use the bathroom."
I tore them up right there   and flushed them down
    the toilet.
When I got home Xander saw me sad and asked,
        "Where'd all your cutouts go?"
I didn't look at him when I said,
        "I don't like them no more."

He knew I was lying. Xander *always* knows when I'm
    lying.
But I lied anyway because
Nara was my best friend and her opinion mattered
                                    over mine
                                    somehow.

63. SOMEONE

Someone is knocking at the front door,
but Mom's at the hospital and I'm lying down
on Xander's bed,
knotted
like a pretzel.
His pillow against my chest.
Rivers escape my eyes
through blurred lenses, as I look at his
shelves of trophies and medals.
I squeeze my eyes shut
hoping that it's all a dream.

                        The knocks grow louder.
                        My heart beats faster.

The detectives, maybe? I'm scared because I'm learning
that not everyone can be trusted.
I get up
pillow against my chest,
half walk and half dread
as I head through the living room.
I put my ear against the front door.
"Who is it?" I almost whisper.
"Ray Ray, it's me."
The pillow drops from my arms.
Dad?

64. DAD HAS HIS EYES

"You all right today, Ray Ray?"
"Mm-hmm."
Dad has eyes like Xander's,
I didn't recognize it until just now.
When he looks up
        I see them.
What Mom calls   *those fake brown eyes*
because like Xander's eyes

it looks like his eyes are dark brown
like me and Mom's,
but when the light hits,
they become the color of honey.

Suddenly his cheeks are X's cheeks,
and his nose is X's nose
and his lips are X's lips.
Even his forehead looks like my brother's.
All of a sudden
I feel sad and look away.
Oh yeah, he's our *dad,* right? X *should* look like his
    dad.
He sits there and I sit there,   waiting for Mom to get
    here,
to make sense of whatever this is.

I don't know what to do   or say,
so many unspoken things between us.
"Me and your mother," he starts again.
"We're trying to make sure that your brother's all right."
We're?
            "Yeah, I know."
            "I went to see him yesterday."
            "You did?"
I wonder what that was like for Xander,   for Mom.

"Yes."

I nod, praying for the ceiling to fall in on me.

The front door opens to a surprised Mom.

When Mom starts talking to Dad,

I go to my room.   I close the door.   I lie down on
my bed.

> *Something inside me wants nothing to do with him.*
> *Something inside me is glad he remembered me.*

I hear the front door close and there's a knock on my
bedroom door.

"Rain?" Mom opens the door,   walks in, and sits
on my bed

but I'm too weak to sit up

because I know she's going right back to work.

To work the night shift   leaving me to face the
night all alone.

"Mommy," I mutter.

She touches my hair.

"I promise to brush your hair tomorrow." She yawns

"I spoke to your dad, and he's asking to see you and
Xander more."

"Xander's not even home yet." I feel kind of angry. I
pause. "Why?"

She shrugs.

"Guilt? Everything's just been . . ." She rubs her
forehead. "I didn't know he was coming."

"It's okay," I whisper.
"Okay, baby, get some rest."

She kisses my cheek and leaves,
and a thousand tears wash away her kiss.

65. JOURNAL

I don't know how I'm supposed to feel when Dad
comes around.
Should I be happy that he's here?
Should I be sad because of what it took for him
to be here?

66. NARA'S OVER AGAIN

"He's even a hashtag, girl."
I'm zoned out. *Huh?*
"What?"
She sits on top of my bed and shoves her phone in my
        face.
"Xander! Xander's a hashtag."
I push her phone away.
"Hashtag? He's not even dead."
"Well, he *could've* died."
She says it so quick.   I'm stunned
        and speechless   and I wonder
about the last time she asked how X was doing.

I don't tell her that my dad was here.
I don't want to tell her anything.

                    I'm used to her not knowing anything
                                about me anyway.
I don't even know if she's really what a friend
is supposed to be.

67. DISGUSTED

I check the social media that
Mom forbids me to have and see that Nara posted
a whole post   *and photo*   of me
along with her and X,
from my seventh birthday party   at school.
I'm wearing a pink dress because Mommy made it
    princess themed.
But I didn't feel like a princess.
And in the photo Xander's clowning,
holding my birthday crown over his head
and I'm laughing at him
holding on to him for dear life.   *I guess not much has*
    changed.
Nara is cheesing so hard with icing on her face.

Nara has over one hundred likes on the photo.
Instead of feeling supported

                              I'm disgusted.

68. JOURNAL

Nara just doesn't get it.

How, after all these years, does she not get it?
How does she not get me?

How can someone who's known me for so long still
not understand me?

Is that her fault?

Or mine?

69. SUPPOSED TO FEEL

"Rain, Xander's coming home tomorrow."
My eyes widen. My heart stops.
"He is?"
I'm excited and scared at the same time.
I've missed my brother so much.
and feel so broken by him not being   home.
"He is, baby, he is."

Tears are running down her face,
and her tears
make me cry too.

70. TODAY'S THE DAY

Xander's coming home.

        Xander's coming home.
        Xander's coming home.
        Xander's coming home.
        Xander's coming home.
        Xander's coming home.

I can't believe it.   I could explode.

        Xander's coming home.
        Xander's coming home.
        Xander's coming home.
        Xander's coming home.
        Xander's coming home.

I sit in the living room and wait for Mom to bring my
    brother back to us.

The door opens
and there he is.

71. PRACTICED THIS

"Xander!"
I run to him and hug him as gentle as I can
to not hurt him   although
                              I wish I could hug him tighter than
                                      I've ever hugged him.
Tighter than after a game,
than on his birthday
than on Christmas morning.

                    But he doesn't hug me back.
                    He doesn't even lift his arms.
                    He doesn't say a word.
                    He doesn't smell the same.
                         I look up into his bruised face
                              to see if it's really him.
His face is *cold*.
Mom puts her hand on his back and walks him into his
      room.
She helps him lie down.

I stand by his bedroom door   and watch   with
    so much to say
and so much to ask.
But he just closes his eyes
and lies there.
Like he didn't just come home.
Like he didn't just see me.

Maybe I should tell a joke.
"Come on, Rain."
"But Mommy . . ."
She closes his bedroom door
and we walk into the living room.
I sit down and look at her as she laces her sneakers.
She looks at me with eyes so sunken
I'm not sure if they're hers.
"He's tired, Rain. Xander has to rest."
I bite my bottom lip.
"Okay."

She stands up. Mom is working a double. I won't see her
    until tomorrow.
"Remember, Rain, if he needs help, help him. If you
    need help, call me."
I nod. We've practiced this.
"Mom, you're gonna leave when he just came back?"

She puts her hand on her forehead.
"Rain, I have to work, you know I have to."

I sit and wait in the living room for my brother   but
he stays in his room for the rest of the night   maybe
he's tired like Mom says.

72. THE NEXT DAY

I sit in the living room,
waiting for X to come out.
Mom walks through the front door.
"He didn't come out?"
I look up at her and she knows my answer.
"He's tired," she says.
I'm wondering how many more times
she'll have to say it.
I nod for her sake.
"Yeah, he is."

73. I'M BACK AT SCHOOL

And I just don't want to be here.
Mom comes with me to speak to the principal,
because it's protocol for a parent
to show up when their children are
                    b r o k e n.
When the principal looks at me   I feel like dirt.
Everyone   in the halls   staring at me like
    something's
wrong with me.
                              And they're right.

74. I WALK PAST

At home I walk past the open bathroom door.
Xander's pulling a shirt over his head
and I see his back,
which has black and dark blue
     bruises
all over.
Oh my God.

     "Xander," I gasp.
He jumps, turning around,
pulling down his shirt,
kicking the
door closed
with his
              foot.

75. IN MISS WALIA'S ENGLISH CLASS

I sit quietly.   Miss Walia treats me normally, except
for the side eye she gives me the entire time.
She doesn't call on me to do anything except breathe.
          "You okay, Rain?" she whispers as she walks
                    past my desk.
My head is down.
                              I exhale into my arm.
          "Yes."

When handing out a vocabulary worksheet, she asks,
          "You sure you're okay, Rain?"
I nod.

When helping someone behind me with their writing,
     she asks,
          "Need anything, Rain?"
I shake my head *no*.

When the bell rings, she walks beside me all the way
     into the hallway.

"I'm okay," I say first.
She nods   although
she still has a worried look on her   face.

76. SAME QUESTION

Nara is mad at me for ignoring her texts and calls.
After class she has a lot of questions,
but I don't have any answers.

"Who are those people that beat up X?"
Beat up X   makes my chest hurt.

"I don't know."

"What you mean, you don't know?"

She thinks I'm lying.

She thinks I'm keeping some secret.

Something juicy.

Something she could *post* about.

77. COLD SHOULDERS

Nara and I don't speak at all, and it's awkward.
She has friends but I don't.
She has Dante in her pocket,
I have loose Skittles in mine.
I think Miss Walia notices.
I don't know how it happened.
The days are long
                with cold shoulders.

78. MY FAULT

In science class I hear Nara talking and laughing
with her friends in the back.
I wish the beanie that I wear every day could cover my
    whole face.
I swear it feels like small blades are pressing into my
    chest.
I hold my pencil tight and look down at the worksheet,
holding back tears.
        "Hey."
I look up to see Alyssa, who lost her *unassigned but usual*
    seat to Nara,
and wouldn't ask for it back.
        "Hey," she says again.
I'm afraid of what she will say next,
until she sits down and takes out her notebook,
and quietly copies the assignment from the board.

The next morning, Amare sits in front of me with his
    breakfast tray,
as I put my head down, far away from Nara's table.

How did he even see me?

"Rain."

"Yeah." My sleeve's in my mouth, saliva-
soaked.

"You okay?"

I don't have strength to answer,
so I just fall

asleep.

79. WHEN MOM LEAVES

When Mom leaves for her night shift
my heart feels like a drum trying to beat

out of my chest.

I know all the bills are high but
I turn on all the lights   *that I can.*
Even that freaks me out   because it's so
unnatural.

The night that took my brother away   now
takes my mother.

I sit on the floor of my bedroom   and rock
                back and forth.

I can't breathe.
I can't sleep.

                        I can't do this anymore.

80. I WAIT

I wait for the sun to come up to fall asleep,
but that doesn't really work
when you've got to get dressed for school.

I'm weak and tired.

At lunch I walk the hallways
to avoid Nara and her crew in the cafeteria.
I pace back and forth with my bag on.
            "Rain?"
I look up to see Miss Walia.

She doesn't ask any questions.
"You can stay with me in my classroom," she
says. "During lunch."

In Miss Walia's classroom
I put my head down on my desk and sleep until the bell
rings   and lunch is over.

81. REAL FORGOTTEN

At church, I'm sweating.
At church, the pastor says
that God never forgets us, but
all I'm feeling is *real* forgotten lately.

I lean my head down to where Xander's shoulder used
to be.

Mom goes up for prayer and falls to her knees at the
altar.
I want to run to her, to tell her everything's going to be
okay,

but I can't even convince myself.
So instead I'm holding my face in my hands,
wishing everything   *especially me*

                                    could disappear.

Everyone sees us.

        Even here   my thoughts   still scream.

82. WHEN I GET HOME

When I get home from school
I go into the bathroom and scratch my face   with
    my fingernails

                                    on purpose.
I didn't mean to do it.

        Well, yeah, I *meant* to do it
but I didn't *want* to hurt myself
but I feel so disgusting   so *disgusted*   with me
    with life.
I'm
so
upset

                so I do it   and it feels right.

83. THE NEXT MORNING

Mom looks at me.

       "Rain, what happened to your face?"

She walks up to me and holds my face.

My chest tightens.

      "Let me get something for that." She rushes

         into the bathroom.

My heart beats faster.

She comes back with ointment.

She starts dabbing it gently on my face with her finger.

      "Do it like this." She hands it to me. "But,

        baby, what happened? Could it be—"

Her phone rings.

        She exhales,   then answers,

    "Yes, Detective Foster,"

and walks into the bathroom to speak with him.

84. SHE MEANS IT

I go into the girls' bathroom at school   when it's
       empty,
and cry a little too loud because I know I am alone.
But when I walk out of the stall
I see Alyssa.
She hands me a napkin for my face and walks out.

In science class Alyssa leans over to me and whispers,
              "I'm sorry about what happened to your
                     brother,"
and because she means it
I walk out of class to wipe my tears.

85. UNYOKED

Quiet Xander
is a whole new person.

Show me ID
show me a birth certificate.
Because I don't recognize this quiet X,
this distant X, at all.

Once he finally comes out of his room,
I watch him play with his cereal at the kitchen table.
I see how his mouth has become an egg
afraid to crack open,
to show life.

Guarded
protected
inside,
unyoked with everything and everyone around him.
But in some ways so am I.

86. JOURNAL

Who do you tell when everything hurts?
What do you say?
When do you say it?
Where do you say it?
Why is it worth saying?
How does it help?

87. I FEEL A TAP

I feel a tap on my shoulder.
"You don't eat lunch?"
I turn around and it's Alyssa.
"Uhh . . ."
"I don't see you in the cafeteria anymore.
Where do you go?"

I look down at my hands.

> "I . . . uhh . . . go to Miss Walia's room during
> lunch."

> "To do work?"

> "Yeah," I lie.

> "*Ohhhh*, okay. So you're going there today
> too?"

I look over my shoulder to see if Miss Walia is standing
in front of her door yet.

> "You could come sit with me and my friend
> at lunch if you want to eat lunch before
> you go to Miss Walia's room."

Really? Me?

Alyssa is smiling wide.

I smile a little too   at her kindness.

Maybe I should go to the cafeteria for a change.

I look over my shoulder for Miss Walia one more time.

> "Oh, okay, yeah."

My heart beats faster as I dread seeing Nara again.

88. I FOLLOW ALYSSA INTO THE CAFETERIA

And she walks in the opposite direction of
where Nara and her crew sit   where I *used* to sit.
Thank God.

I still can't stop shaking.

We walk up to a table where a boy with a familiar face
    is standing.
                "Rain, this is Umi. Umi, this is Rain."
                "Hey." I sit as Alyssa sits. I know Umi from
                    elementary school.
                "Wassup, Rain?"
He looks at Alyssa and says,
                "Yeah, I know Rain. She rolls with the cool
                    kids."
I shrug.
                "Not really."
He looks up at me   eyebrows kind of scrunched

kind of confused until he nods

kind of apologetically and says,

"Aiight."

He sits down and takes out a notebook.

"Y'all doing work at lunch?"

He laughs.   "Nah."

Alyssa says, "He's just writing some stuff for after-
     school. You should join after-school."

Nara and I *never* joined any after-school program.

Who would want to stay at school for an

     extra   *three hours?*

"Nah, I'm good."

And I sit there quietly, wondering why I came.

89. LEMON

I look at Dad,
finally realizing that I look like him   too.
His eyes look sad
filled with some kind of sorrow.

                    I guess he's really part of the family.
        "Hey, Ray Ray."
        "Hey, Dad."
I have to get used to this whole *Dad* thing,
the word *Dad* feels like a lemon pressed against my
    tongue.
I sit across from him   on the living room sofa   with
    my feet up.

He's here to see Xander,
who I haven't seen come out of his room   in twenty-
    four hours.
He asks me about school   my classes   my friends.
He asks what I like to do   my hobbies   what I'm
    good at.

He asks how X is doing   *as if I know*   as if anyone
    truly knows.

Everything's just   too awkward   too painful.
                                I wish Mom was home.
                           I wish *home* felt like home.

"Let me see if X is up."

I get up and walk to Xander's door.

I put my ear against it   try to hear any
    sound   any movement   any*thing*.
           "Xander," I say. "Xander, it's Rain."

I stand there   listening   waiting   breathing
    with my eyes closed,

hoping   he'll open   the door   and wrap his
    long arm around my neck and say,
          Wassup, Rain-drop!

But he doesn't.
        "Ray Ray?" It's Dad.

I walk back and he's standing at the front door with his
    coat on.

Before Dad leaves, he asks,
        "Are you good, Ray-Ray? Do you need
           anything?"

There's nothing in the fridge. I'm still wearing X's old
    hoodies.

I have no more hair supplies.

But why does he care?   *Does he even care for real?*
      "I'm okay."

90. SHAKING

Xander's friends are over.
They're like Mom's other sons,
and today   their pain proves that.

Especially Butter.
          "Hey, Rain."
          "Wassup, Rain."
          "Yo, Rain, what's good?"
They all walk in drenched from the snow.
Mom woke up for this   for them   for this moment.
Mom has been sleeping more and more   again.

After they take their coats and boots off
Mom brings them into X's room,
hoping this will make him *more like him*   somehow.
But when I peek in, Xander looks like he's in so much
      pain.
They don't know what to do with him.
          Me neither.

They just lean in for hugs and walk out.
"What's happening with those clowns?" Dre Dre. "The
    ones who hurt X?"
"He's *still* hurt," Jay says. Everyone's shaking their head.
I'm now looking on from the kitchen   afraid to get
    too close.

Mom crosses her arms over her chest, looking more
    tired than ever.

"They got them, they got all the boys."
"About time." Butter. "If it was one of us, they would've
    gotten us . . ."
"The same night," I say.

And everybody looks at me in silence, and the sadness
rises so strong inside that I can't stop my leg from
    shaking.

91. AT THE CENTER

Mr. Jackson pulls me aside
at school for a second.
"Rain, how's Xander doing?"
His favorite student ever.
I look up at him.
"He's okay."

I'm not sure, and he can tell.
He reads it off me like a textbook.

"Okay," he replies, but it's more of a question than a
    statement.
Shouldn't adults know not to put kids
                    at the center
                    of it all?

92. I'M SICK

I'm sick, but I don't say it.
My head spins, my tummy beats against my insides.
I want to throw up.
I just hate feeling like this.
Everything feels like my fault.

"Rain," Miss Walia calls.
My face presses against the cool of the desk.

> *You're ugly.*
> *You're not good enough.*
> *Nobody likes you.*
> *Only bad things will happen.*

"Rain, are you okay?"
I open my mouth, but nothing comes.
I try again.
"Yes."
Too much is happening for me
to be sick.

93. AT LUNCH

The next day
I sit across from Alyssa and Umi in the cafeteria
before I go to Miss Walia's classroom.
Despite how sad I feel
somehow they make me laugh,
        Umi always cracking jokes about
    his teachers   Alyssa always having
      some funny story about her family.
They seem not to notice
what I look like   what I wear
my lack of words   or at least they
don't say anything.
"My math teacher really had the audacity to talk in my
    face with that breath of his." Umi.
I laugh.
"How bad was it?" Alyssa asks.
He looks at me.
"You ever change a baby's diaper?"
We all bust out laughing.

"Umi, that's not nice." Alyssa takes out her lunch, which
    looks more like dinner. "Rain, try this."
"No, it's—"
She puts it in my hand anyway. Something wrapped
    like a taco, but not quite.
I bite into it.
"Good, no?"
She smiles and Umi eats like it's his last meal.
"Rain." Alyssa snaps me out of thought.
"It's good, thank you," I say.
"*Mad* good." Umi licks his fingers. "But ain't nothing
    better than my grandma's fried chicken! Wait,
    Alyssa, is Rain pulling up to Josiah's birthday party
    or nah?"
Alyssa shrieks. I jump, a little   nervous.
Huh?
"My brother Josiah is turning"—she holds her hand
    up—"five. And we're throwing a birthday party for
    him. You should come!"
Me?
"I . . . uhh . . ."
"Yeah, you should, my pops could bring us." Umi.
"I'll ask my mom," I say.
Did I just say that?
Alyssa applauds like I'm a baby that just walked for the
    first time.

Umi shakes his head, laughing.

I smile.

"Oh, Rain." Umi pulls a paper from his book bag.

"I thought of you today when I saw this."

Thought of me? Got to be something bad.

He puts it down.   It's a flyer   *the* flyer   for the
    step team tryouts.

"Rain, you step?!" Alyssa.

"No, I . . ."

"Yeah you do." Umi squints at me. "Or you did. In
    elementary school."

"I'll do it with you!" Alyssa. "It'll be cool."

"Yeah, why not?" Umi.

"I don't know if I'd be good at it anymore," I admit.

"I think you will be." Umi.

"Same." Alyssa.

I nod   unsure.

But it's

nice to

have people

            believe in me

                even when I struggle to believe in myself.

94. THAT NIGHT

I try to think of ways to tell
Alyssa and Umi that   I *can't*   sit with them at lunch,
because I'm   *too behind on homework*   *yes, work.*
  Something inside me   makes me feel like hiding away
                              from everyone   again.
When I see Umi in the hallway the next day, I'm ready
    to tell him.
"Umi, I—"
"Rain, it's just you and me today. Alyssa's mom is sick."
"Sick?"
He looks past me. "Yeah." He pauses. "So, you coming?"
I nod   unsure,   but I walk with him anyway.

In the cafeteria, when I sit across from Umi,
Xander's hoodie   *the one I wear every day*   is making
    me sweat more than usual.
I'm nervous   realizing
that I'm more comfortable with Umi when Alyssa's
    around.

He pulls candy from his pocket.

Sour candy,   which is my favorite.

"You want some?"

I shake my head.

"No, I'm good."

"So what's good with you and Nara?"

I look over in the direction where Nara and her crew
    are sitting *where I used to sit.*

"I guess we're just . . . just not friends anymore."

I look at him.   He nods, eating his candy.

"Is it because of the whole thing with your brother?"

I feel sick at the mention of Xander.

"My brother's fine."

Which isn't the truth,   but he nods anyway.

"That's good."

I nod too   grateful   that Umi doesn't pull
    painful explanations   out of me.

I don't think he believes me, though.

95. XANDER'S CASE

Although I try to ignore it, and Mom tries to hide it,
Xander's case is still not over.

When they come back from the millionth trip
    of meeting with lawyers
they both look sad.
Did they find out who hurt X?
Are they being charged?
I want to ask   but I'm afraid to.
X walks right into his room,   without saying a word.
Mom walks into the kitchen, opens the fridge, and
    sighs,
                "Rain, I'll be back."
My stomach starts to ache.
                "Okay."
Everything feels so cold.

I get my journal.

96. JOURNAL

I feel so bad for Mommy sometimes for everything she has to do for us. Maybe two kids are just too much for her. Xander is the one who needs her the most right now. Maybe Xander should've been the only kid she had. Maybe I'm just too much.

97. ALL OF A SUDDEN

I hear a loud sound,
then another one,
and another,

banging
something hitting
hard.
"Mommy!" I scream. Although she's not here.

I jump up   *panting*

                sweating and run to the sound *that sound*

                            coming from a room.

                                        Xander's room.

I push open his door.

"Xander!"

X is throwing his trophies, and my eyes open wide like

                    a deer in headlights,

                one I've never seen in real life,

                one I've only read about or seen on TV.

"Xa-Xa-Xander!"

I run into the kitchen to call 9-1-1 when the front door

    opens.

"Mommy, Xander!"

She looks at me,   drops the bags in her hands,

then runs into his room.

I follow behind her   screaming

Mom runs up to Xander and tries to stop his arms

    his strong arms

from throwing and breaking his trophies.

No no no no no no no no no no.

"Xander, stop it!" she screams. *"Stop it!"*

Now I'm on the floor

                    on the floor   begging

"Xander, please stop, please!"

She holds his hands   and suddenly, he stops

and he's   breathing heavily   full of sweat,
staring at the ground   half of a trophy in his hand.
Mom wraps her arm around his neck,   pulling him
          into her,
as tears roll down his face.

98. I RUN

I run into my room and cry.
Mom showers without the light on   like she used
          to   when we lived in the shelter.
She has to leave for work.

"Mommy, no, *please no*," I beg as she laces her sneakers.
"Rain," she says, her eyes bloodshot. "I have to work. I
          can't afford any of this."
Any of this. My throat suddenly feels dry, but I muster,
"Okay."
Mom tries to put on a small smile,   her usual sacrifice.
"I do this for *us*," she reminds me. *Us.*

99. AT NIGHT I ASK

God, why is this happening?
Why is this happening to us?

I get out of bed and go to the bathroom.
I look at myself in the mirror   thinking,

I'm nothing. I'm nothing. I'm nobody.

And I can't stop. I can't stop thinking like this.

I don't feel safe anymore.
Not even from myself.

100. WHEN WE WERE YOUNGER

Sometimes Xander and I would go to work with Mom
    on random weekends when
X didn't have practice   or a game.
                     Which didn't happen often.

We'd take the bus *way* outside the City,
to where she would clean houses in the real nice
    neighborhoods.
"I do this for the both of you," Mom would say with a
    tired smile. "For *us*."

X and I would run around the house she'd be cleaning
up and down the stairs, pretending like we owned the
    place,
deciding which room would be ours.
"This room is bigger. I want it!"
I would try to block him from entering, but of course
    Xander was way stronger.
"Nah, Rain-drop, this one would be mine."

Then I'd pout, like it was a real-life decision.
"Fine, fine, you can have it." He'd pause. "One day
     Imma buy a house *way* bigger than this one!"
"When you're a pro athlete, right?"
He shrugged. "When I'm anything." *Anything?*

I'd question his response for a millisecond
before I got all excited and squeezed him real tight,
because I truly believed him.

Xander would save us.

101. TODAY THERE'S A MATH TEST

Today there's a math test, but I haven't studied.

When Mr. B puts the test down on my desk,
I just stare at it, while everybody else works.

Math is so foreign to me
I think I need a passport to understand it.

102. DAD IS BACK

Dad is back, and Mom doesn't look like Mom.
She looks

broken
sad
lost.

Dad's here to try to speak to Xander.
Mom told him about X's latest incident.
Xander's two for two on incidents.
Dad looked real serious, like he's done this before,
as if he's the best one to help Xander.
Maybe he has before.
Maybe it was just too long ago for me to remember.

I stand in the hallway and watch as Dad goes to hug
    Xander.
Xander doesn't even lift his arms.

103. MOM SAYS

"Your dad wants to take you out this weekend."

"Out? Out where?"

She shrugs. "He said the movies or something."

Movies? I only go to the movies when Nara's parents are
*   paying for it.*

She sits on my bed. "What do you think? You don't have
    to go if you don't want to."

I shrug. "I guess I could go."

Mom's face isn't too pleased, but she's desperate.

    I am too.

"Okay."

104. JOURNAL

Me + Dad + Movies = ????

105. MISS WALIA

Miss Walia tells me to stay back after class and I'm
    feeling like some type of delinquent.
"Rain."
"Yeah?" I don't look up.
"I've been trying to give you space, with everything
    that's happened with Xander.
But Rain, I'm worried about you."
I look down at the desk.
"Rain, look at me."
I look up, feeling embarrassed, feeling like nothing.
"Do you even hear anything I say in class?"

I shake my head. "No." *Not in any of my classes*
I want to say.

She brings her face closer to mine. "Rain, breathe, you
need to breathe."
So I try and with every breath, I realize how much she's
right,
how I *don't* breathe, how much I hold everything in.
"That's it, inhale, exhale, breathe."

106. XANDER

Xander is getting ready to leave,
to go back to school   for the first time   since the
incident.
"Good morning," I say to him in the cheeriest voice I
got.
"Good morning."
"How was your sleep? Are you excited about today?" I
ask with a wide smile.
He shrugs.

He looks at me   and holds the gaze longer than
   usual.
Mom is walking around him   fixing
    him   freaking out   a bit.
                                                          I am too.
She wraps a scarf around his neck. It's snowing pretty
    hard today.
"You okay getting there on your own, Xander?"   Her
    dream. Her dread.
"Yeah." His voice is barely audible   as usual.
"Bye, Xander," I say.
I look up at him from the kitchen table   with tears
    in my eyes
when he doesn't   say goodbye.

107. CIRCLE GROUP

"Rain." I pick my head up off the desk in Miss Walia's
    class.
"Yes?" I wipe the drool from the side of my cheek.

I'm at school early and didn't want to wait in the
     cafeteria   with everyone else.

She pulls up a chair and sits next to me. She puts papers
     down in front of me.
"In after-school . . . there's this activity with the school
     counselor and me. It's called Circle Group. It's a
     blend of writing and discussion. It's very helpful for
     students who . . . go through things. I think you'll
     benefit from it. Here are the forms that your mom
     needs to fill out and then you can start right away. I
     think this will be good for you, Rain. I think you'll
     really enjoy it."
"I don't . . ."
"Rain, just try it out."

108. MOM

Mom is half-asleep
in her work clothes
when she signs my papers for after-school.

109. I DON'T TELL

I don't tell Alyssa and Umi about the after-school thing
  yet.

Maybe if it goes well   I'll tell them.

110. I WALK INTO THE GYM

Which now consists of a circle of chairs
and students talking to each other.
I'm sweating and my heart is racing.
Is it too late to run?

Miss Walia leads me to an empty seat
and I keep my eyes on my lap.
"Rain." I look up.

"I'm Dr. McCalla, and I'm a counselor here at City
    Middle School. It's so great to have you here with us
    at Circle Group."
He smiles at me.
I nod and return my gaze to my lap. I'm praying myself
    invisible.
"Okay, guys, let's get settled," Miss Walia says.
The seats get filled up,   but I still can't look up
    because
someone is sitting to my right and my left. *Oh God.*

"How's everyone doing today?" Dr. McCalla.
"Good," says everyone but me.
I nod a little   because *I'm not feeling too good.*
Not yesterday   not today   not here   not now.
"We have someone new with us today. Someone joining
    Circle Group."
I look to my right slightly,   then wave
then put my gaze back   into my lap.
They clap   *for me? Why?*

"Okay, cool, kids." Miss Walia. "Let's get some roses and
    thorns of the day . . . maybe the week . . . month . . .
    year? You choose. The floor is yours."

"Well," a voice starts. "My thorn is still my stepfather.
    And how angry he used to get at my mom . . . at

us. Although he's not there anymore, I mean, the damage is still done, you know? It's weird because my little brother's always asking for him. It's his real dad, so I don't really know what to say to him."

They have dad issues, too?

"Thank you for sharing."

"My rose." Another voice. "Today. Today is my rose. Today is a better day. Yesterday I was really low about my sister not being home anymore. That she *chose* to leave. That she *chose* that life."

She feels low, too?

"Thank you for sharing."

"Anyone else want to share their rose? Their thorn?" Dr. McCalla.

"I'll go." *That voice sounds familiar.*

"Well, most of you guys know I come from an undocumented household, and it's not easy. Both of my parents are undocumented. My dad works a lot of different odd jobs. My mom does as well. I worry about them. My mom got sick recently—which was my thorn. She doesn't have insurance, so her getting sick is real tough on my family, on me. But she's been doing better now—which is my rose. We're a lot happier now."

"Thank you for being our last share-out, Alyssa." Miss Walia.

Alyssa?! I look up, and directly across from me is Alyssa
    and next to her is Umi.
I look back down   my heart pounding out of my
    chest.
How did they get so bold to tell the truth?
I need to get out of here.
I can't stop my whole body from shaking.

111. I TRY TO GET OUT

I try to get out of Circle Group quickly   once it's over.
"Rain!" Alyssa says.
"Yo, *Rain!*" says Umi.
But I pretend like I don't hear them and leave the
    building as

                fast

           as

              I

               can.

112. JOURNAL

I don't think Circle Group is for me.

113. WHEN WE WERE YOUNGER

Xander would not only save the fruit he got from his
    own lunch,
but would ask his friends and teammates for *their* fruit
that they never ate and stuff it into his book bag.

When he'd get home, he would pour it all out and we'd
    eat it,
        just in case Mom was sleeping   again,
        just in case Mom wasn't able to cook   again.

"X, you okay?" I'd ask. His face looked a way I'd never
    seen before.
"I just don't get why Mom . . ."
"Mom, what?"
He'd hand me the fourth tangerine he'd finished
    peeling.
"Nothing, nothing."

114. DODGING

I try to dodge Alyssa and Umi
the next day,   but it's nearly impossible.
"Rain!" Alyssa runs up to me and gives me the biggest,
    warmest hug. "I'm so glad you're a part of Circle
    Group! Isn't it awesome?"
Why is she so nice to me?
I feel happy and sad all at once.
"It's okay."
"Sit with us next time, okay?"
I don't know.
"Okay."

115. I'M BACK

I'm back at Circle Group, even though I don't know if I
    want to be here.
I debated with Miss Walia as to why I shouldn't come.
But she wasn't having it.
"But I . . . I don't want to say anything."
"You don't have to, Rain."

Today I feel obliged to sit next to Alyssa and Umi,
although I wish no one could see me

                                        at all.

I barely pay attention until Dr. McCalla asks,
"And what makes a good Circle Group?"
People start calling out.
            "Honesty."
            "Openness."
            "Feeling safe."
            "Trust."
            "Yes!" Dr. McCalla turns my way. "Trust is
                very important."

"Today," he continues, "we'll be doing the trust
    challenge. Some of you remember how to do it
    from last time. Find a partner, catch a partner, then
    switch!"
Catch a partner?
"Wanna be my partner, Rain?"
I look up. It's Umi.
I turn to see where Alyssa is   but she's already paired
    up.
"I'm too big for this."
"Too *big?*"
I nod   afraid to say it again   and then he'll *really* notice.
"Nah, come on. Let's try it."
It takes me a moment before I stand up.
"I . . . I'll catch you first."
He smiles.
"No problem."
He stands in front of me   facing away from me
    a bit of distance away.
I hold out my arms   then he falls back
    effortlessly
and I catch him.
"Okay, Rain, now Imma catch you."
I want to run and hide somewhere
                but I can't,
so I stand where he stood.
"Okay, Rain, you can fall back now."

But
I can't.
       "Rain?"
I turn around.
       "I . . . Sorry . . . I just . . ."
He puts both his hands up.
"No worries, it's cool. Next time."

Although I feel embarrassed, I say,
"Thank you,"
because I am also *relieved* that he didn't force
    it   didn't press it.

He smiles at me and I

       smile back.
Thanks, Umi.

116. FACE-TO-FACE

I come face-to-face with Nara
walking down the hall with her friends.
They're looking at me and whispering   laughing
about me.

117. WHEN I GET HOME

When I get home,
I force myself not to

                        eat.

118. MOM'S ROOM

I go into Mom's room   well, my room
        the room we share.   I go into our closet
        and take money from her coat pocket,
where she keeps the rent. Then I leave
        because   *Xander doesn't care anyway.*
It's freezing but I walk all the way to the hair store.
I walk through one aisle,
                a second aisle,
                a third aisle,
until I see them. The women.
The women on the jars with the
clear   light   bright   beautiful skin.
                                        Unlike mine.
I grab the jar with the woman with the lightest skin.
I walk up to the cashier, who doesn't look like
        me   *sweating*
wondering if I'm about to get in some trouble,
until he takes the cash and puts the jar into a plastic
        bag.

119. CREAM

I rub the cream
on my knees   on my elbows
under my armpits   on my neck
and it stinks so bad.
I rub it on my face
                    all over my face.
I check the bathroom door to make sure it's locked.
                    But no one is checking on me.

120. THE NEXT DAY

I wake up
terrified,
wondering,
      What did I do?

I run to the bathroom
to see my face.
To see if it's changed.
If I'm
      lighter-skinned   *better*-skinned
but nothing.
I'm afraid that it will happen   out of nowhere   at
    school
when I least expect it   somehow.

121. WHEN WE WERE YOUNGER

Nara would be the one to defend me from bullies,
when Xander wasn't around.
It was real easy for her,
because she was popular,   she was cool,
she was friends with everybody,   even those who
    tried to bully me.

When they'd try to come at me
for my hair
my weight
my dark skin
my old clothes,   *Xander's* old clothes,
she'd be right there to say,
"Leave Rain alone."

She didn't have to yell because
she was *pretty* and her
family had *money*
so people *respected* her and
listened to her.

When Xander would get home from practice,
he'd see me looking kind of down.
"What's wrong?" he'd ask.
"Nothing."
"Aiight, I know you're lying, Rain-drop."
It was hard for me to say anything.

122. MOM'S BRAIDING MY HAIR

Mom's braiding my hair because
Dad is coming to take me to the movies.
I'm so nervous.
She does it at the kitchen table and although I'm close
    to her,
there's a distance between us.
She yawns and combs,
yawns and combs.

Everything just feels so empty.
"Rain," she says. And I think she's going to say
    something about Dad,
or worse   about me.
But instead she says,

"The guys that hurt Xander are being charged with
     assault."

My heart stops. *Charged? Like jail?*
Mom rarely says anything about X.
About those who hurt him.
"Oh," I mumble. "Are all of them . . ."
". . . white?" She pauses. "Yes, they were all white."
Her voice feels so cold.
I want to say something   anything,
but nothing comes out.
I have so many   questions   unanswered.

123. NORMAL SOMEHOW

It's quiet for a long while
as Mom braids my hair.
"So, Mommy." I pause. "My . . . uhh . . . friend from
    class . . . Alyssa. Her family's having a birthday party
    for her little brother. His name is Josiah. And he's
    turning five, I think. And she . . . invited me . . ."
To be honest, I don't really want to go, but I was hoping
    bringing this up
would make things normal somehow.
"Alyssa?"
"Yeah, this girl from my class."
"What happened to Nara? You never mention her
    anymore."
"I . . . she . . . we don't really talk."
"How come?"
The doorbell rings and me and Mom exhale at the
    same time.

124. DAD

I sit in the passenger side of Dad's car
and I just keep thanking God
that the radio makes its own noise.
That it talks *for* us.

We get to the movie theater
and it feels so weird being here.
"What movie do you want to see, Ray Ray?"
We're on the line for the tickets
and I'm standing far enough away from him
that it looks like I came with another family.
I look up and point to one of the advertisements, a
    comedy.
"I guess that one."
He nods. "Yeah, I was thinking the same thing."

We go to the concession stand
and instead of telling me what I can't have
or what's healthy versus not healthy   *like Nara's*
    family,

he orders a whole bunch of stuff
and carries it into the movie himself.

When the movie starts, we get into some type of flow.
He passes me the popcorn. I pass him the candy.
We swap the nachos, he refills my drink.

We keep laughing,   we can't stop laughing,
at this movie   about a family getting into
      mishaps on a vacation.
I forgot how it feels to laugh like this.

And we actually end up doing that thing I do with
      Xander
when something's really funny,
how we look at each other and end up laughing even
      more.

After the movie   we're still laughing,
and in the car too   we laugh.
"That movie was something else!" he says.
"It was *too* funny," I say.
Slowly forgetting how a few hours ago
he felt like such a   stranger   that I was trying to
      escape from.

He pulls up in front of my home. "Your mom says you're
    graduating this year."
I try not to think about it.
                            About me or Xander graduating.
I look out the window. "Yeah, I am."
My stomach hurts   wondering if he'll ask to come to
    my graduation,
and how everybody'll be asking me how all of a sudden
                                    I have a dad.
"Well, she mentioned that there's a dance and I wanted
    to give her the money for your dress."
I don't want to go to any dance, or wear any dress. The
    offer shakes me up a bit.
"Really?"
"Of course, Ray Ray. This is a big deal and you're my
    daughter."
Daughter   from his mouth
sounds   cold and warm at the same time.
"Oh."

I'm not sure what to say   *or how to feel*   or what
    to do,
except get out the car.
"Bye, Ray Ray!" he calls out through the window.
"Bye, Daddy!" I say, running up the steps.
Daddy? Did I just say that?
I sort of   kind of   don't mind the name Ray Ray
    anymore.

125. AFTER

"How was it?"
Mom asks when she comes home from work.
She walks into my room.
"It wasn't bad."

"So what did—" Her cell phones goes off.
She looks down at it, almost hesitant to answer.
"What happened, Mommy?" She puts her index finger
    up and answers.
"Yes, Detective." And then walks out of the room.

With the room door open, I can see Xander walking out
    of the bathroom.
"Wassup, X!" I call out.
"Nothing much."
"How's school?"
He shrugs. "It's aiight."
"That's good."
"I guess so."

He goes back into his room, closing the door behind him.

126. I HAVEN'T HEARD FROM DAD

I haven't heard from Dad in a few days.
I call him, but nothing.
I feel so sick, for getting so excited to call him.

127. JOURNAL

Dad's not answering my calls. God, why would
you give me a parent that doesn't love me like a
parent should?

128. BACK AT CIRCLE GROUP

I'm back at Circle Group and Miss Walia asks,
"What is a cycle that you want to break in your family?"
And we have to answer clockwise.
Everyone's supposed to give an answer, and I'm
    sweating so hard.
"Alcoholism."
"Poverty."
"Anger issues."
"Giving up too quickly."
"Anxiety."
"Divorce."
It stops at me and I almost faint, until Miss Walia says,
        "Next person."

129. ALYSSA'S FAMILY

Today is Alyssa's brother's birthday party
and Alyssa and Umi come inside our place to meet
    Mom.
"Mommy, this is Alyssa. And this is Umi."
They're both real cordial, but Mom greets them with a
    big, tired smile.
The same smile she gives me when I ask her how work
    is going.

When Umi's dad drops us off at Alyssa's house,
I'm suddenly terrified. "Her family's mad cool," Umi
    says, the mind reader.
I nod and secretly pinch the skin of my wrist.

We walk in,   but the party's already started,
and there's a lot of people,   a lot of music,   and a
    lot of food.
Josiah is running around with cake and cousins.
"Mom, this is Rain." Alyssa's so happy to introduce me.
"Rain!" She gives me a hug and a kiss on the cheek.

I flinch
and Umi laughs and *accepts the love so easily* because
    he's a regular.
That's nice.
I smile.

I sit on a sofa with a plate of food that I'm picking at,
and watch how Alyssa's family loves and celebrates
    hard.
It makes me forget how numb I am.
They sing in another language when cutting Josiah's
    cake.
Even Umi sings with them.
Then all of a sudden, a man walks in and everyone's so
    excited.
Alyssa comes over to me and Umi and says,
"My dad's *finally* home from work."
I ask, "What does your dad do?"
She shrugs. "Everything."

130. THE MIND

Xander is sitting at the kitchen table doing homework.
Everything is too quiet, so I double-dare myself to
    speak to him.
Maybe today will be the day things get better,
and old X will come back to us.   To *me*.
"So . . . how was your day?" I don't feel cheery, but I'm
    trying.
He nods. "It was valid," he says softly.
"Okay, good!"
He keeps reading.   I lift the textbook to see the
    cover of it.
"Oh, the psychology book! The book about the *mind*,
    right?"
"Yup." I stand around and wait for more
until he picks up his books, walks into his room,
and closes the door.

131. SOLVE FOR *X*

Today I have a scheduled meeting with Dr. McCalla.
I look around his office. It's nice, it's clean.
He sits at his desk and I sit across from him.
My hands   sweating   folded in my lap
heart racing   wondering
what he's going to ask me.

"So, Rain."
A pain rises in my chest. "Yeah?"
"Well, first"—he folds his hands—"I'm so happy that
     you've joined us in Circle Group."
He pauses.   I guess for me to say something,   to
     agree, but I can't.
He nods. "Miss Walia speaks so highly of you."
Now it's my turn to nod.
"But she's also very concerned about you. I heard about
     what happened to your brother. I wanted to check
     in with you."
"What do you mean?"
"How are you feeling, Rain?"

I pause to think. I feel many things at once,   all the
    time.
Like a storm.   A *Rain* storm.
The first thing that comes to mind is Xander.
"I'm trying to figure out what's wrong with my brother."
He nods for me to keep talking.
"Xander is not the same Xander that I know. He barely
    talks to me or to anyone. X is so different." I shrug.
"And you want to figure it out?"
"I guess."
"That's understandable. You call him *X*, your brother?"
I nod.
"And you're trying to figure out what's wrong with him?"
I nod again.
"Have you ever heard the term 'solve for *x*' in math?"
"Yes, but I hate math, to be honest."
He laughs. "Well, Rain, you are doing some real-life
    equation solving for your brother. You are trying to
    'solve for *x*.' Mathematically, in order to do that, you
    must find the truth in the equation. And although
    you're trying to do this for your brother, Rain, I
    think it's time you try to uncover your *own* truth."
"My *own truth*?" The words feel like Pop Rocks in my
    mouth.
"Yes, Rain. What is true about *you*?"

132. TODAY IS CIRCLE GROUP

In Circle Group, everyone's sitting, talking,
and I'm dreading what's next.
"Rain, we should go to the mall this weekend. Umi's
   dad can drive us." Alyssa.
I look over at Umi, who's scrolling on his cell phone and
   nodding.
"Yeah," he says. "That's definitely a vibe."
I open my mouth to say   *I might be busy*,
but Miss Walia walks into the middle of the circle.

"Hello, everyone." She's all smiles as usual.
"Hello, Miss Walia," we respond like a choir.
"So." She claps her hands together. "Under each of your
   chairs is a mirror. You can pick it up."
A mirror. I reach under my chair,   and she's right.
"Yeah, you can remove the tape from it," she continues.
"But I want you to hold your mirror up to your face like
   this."

Why? I do it, confused.

"And I want you," she continues, "to get a really good
  look at yourself."

I hate looking at myself.

My big, round face with its bigger features.

My skin that's darker than everybody else's.

*My braids that have started to get frizzy because I'm too
  tired to take care of them.*

"And for the next two minutes, you're going to hold it
  there, while I speak. Got it?"

Everyone is nodding. Everyone but me.

"Look at you. Look at how amazing you are. Look
  at all the things you've overcome. You, yes, you,
  are brilliant. You're a star. You are capable of
  accomplishing great things. Look how beautiful you
  are. You should be so proud . . ."

I am brilliant.

I am a star.

I am capable of accomplishing great things.

Look how beautiful I am.

I should be so proud . . .

She keeps going, but I can no longer do it.

So I put the mirror on my lap and pretend
to scroll through my phone.

133. AT CHURCH

At church the pastor preaches on *loving your neighbor*
and my heart feels cold to the idea,   to just loving
    everybody.
I think of Dad
Nara
Zach.

                     All those people that hurt X.
How?
How can I love them?

134. THEN THE PASTOR SAYS

"In order to love your neighbor, you must first learn to
love yourself."

                                        And all of a sudden
                                        I forget how to breathe.

In order to love someone else
                                I have to love myself first?

I guess   it makes sense.

How can I give away   something

                                that I don't have?

It makes me   wonder,

                                        Do I even
                                        love myself?

135. AT CIRCLE GROUP

I look around the room
to see if I'm the biggest girl.
I feel like I am. I *know* I am.
I still keep my coat on.

"Did you get one?" Umi hands me a piece of paper.
In the center is a greater than/less than sign.
"Okay, everyone." Dr. McCalla. "What's greater than
    what you're facing right now?"
I feel like he's looking at me, so I look down   and
    pretend to write.
"Any volunteers to share?" Miss Walia.
Hands go up. She points to them.
"My faith is greater than my fear."
"My future is greater than my past."
"My hope is greater than my pain."
Umi's hand goes up. "My happiness is greater than my
    sadness."
Sadness?
Umi is sad?
I stuff the paper into my pocket.

136. BEAUTIFUL AS YOU

Umi's dad drives me, Umi, and Alyssa to the mall,
which I hate because *there are mirrors everywhere*.

Umi tries on a silly winter hat.
I laugh and pull it off his head.
"That's ridiculous," I say.
"Sorry, Rain, not everybody can be as beautiful as you,"
    he says.

Beautiful as you.
                As *me*?

137. BACKWARD

Before
I've felt
Like nothing
In me   *My mind feels so backward.*
Rising
Has been
Hurt that
All this
Because of
But can't
To journal
I try
Today

138. DOWN THE TOILET

When I wake up   I feel sick
                     I feel sad
                     I feel dark clouds.

I'm not sure why.
                    I thought I was doing better.

But here I am   somehow   stuck, again.
               Hurting, again.

                       Wiping away tears, again.

When Mom leaves for work
I go into the bathroom and do something I know
    I know
I shouldn't do.
Something I've done before.
Something I've tried to stop.
                   And it hurts. It hurts so bad.

I flush the bloody tissue down the toilet.

And
parts of my arm   sting   from what I did
                    sting so bad.

139. I LIE IN MY BED

I lie in bed and imagine
talking with Xander:

X, you're back!
Of course, I'm always here, Rain-drop! What's up?
To be honest, I'm really, really sad.
Sad? No, you shouldn't be sad! There's nothing
to be sad about!
I know, but I just am. I don't really understand, but it's been
getting worse. Everything hurts.
Rain-drop, don't worry! Big bro is right here!
But, X, I'm worried about you.
About me? How come?
You're not the same person that you used to be.
I'm still here, Rain. I promise.

140. REVEALED

Alyssa's absent today, because her mom is sick again.

I stayed in Miss Walia's class during lunch   trying to
    avoid Umi

but he found me anyway and started walking with me
    outside.

"I'll walk home with you and ask my dad to pick me up
    from your house."

I put my hands in my pockets.

"Why do you even want to walk with me?" I say out
    loud, by accident.

"What do you mean?"

"Like I don't get why you even want to be my . . .
    uhh . . ."

Silence.

"Friend?"

"Yeah."

"Rain, you're not serious, are you?"

He shakes his head like I just asked him why the grass
    is green.

All of a sudden he slips   on ice,
and he grabs my wrist to stop from falling
and I scream so loud,

                                        too loud
                                        because

the cuts hurt.
"Oh my God, Rain, I'm so sorry."
He pushes up the sleeve of my jacket
and looks down to see if he hurt me,
and sees that I already hurt myself.

"Yo, Rain, what happened?"
I don't realize how many cuts there are
until it's revealed in the sun   like this.
He's scared, but I'm more scared. I look into his eyes.
"Please don't tell anyone."
He looks away.
        "I won't."

141. DR. MCCALLA'S OFFICE

I'm sitting in Dr. McCalla's office and I'm nervous
   because I think I'm here because I'm not speaking
   at Circle Group because it's just too overwhelming
   and I just don't know what to say but it's not like I
   don't want to go but it's just too hard for me to say
   anything and now I think I'm getting in trouble
   for it but I don't want to get in trouble but there's
   just so much going on right now both inside and
   outside me.

   "Rain, are you harming yourself?"

142. SLUSH

I walk up to Umi and push him in the chest. "You
    told?!"
Tears are falling from my eyes.
"Yes, Rain. I can't just watch you hurt yourself!"
"You want me to get in *trouble*?!"
"Rain, I don't think you're okay."
"And you are?"
"Come on, Rain!"
I run out of the school.
"Rain!" Alyssa's voice follows me.

I walk home and it's so cold,
and my face, hands, and toes are ice, and I'm crying.
I just want to sit in the middle of the road,
but the cars are moving too slow in this slush.

143. I AM NEVER

I am never
ever
going back to
Circle Group.

144. THE NEXT MORNING

I can't get up, I can't move,
I cry into my pillow, hoping the pain will go away.

But it never does.
There's a *ding* from my phone,
then another.
Probably Alyssa.
Probably Umi.

I throw my phone across the room.

145. LATER THAT NIGHT

Later that night there's a knock on my bedroom door.
"Rain."
I wipe my face with my hands, my head pounding.
I keep my head under the covers.
Mommy?
"Yes—yes, Mommy."
She opens the door and turns the light on.
"I got a call from your school today."
No no no no
God no please no.

"Mommy, I'm feeling kind of sick. My stomach and
    head hurt, so I stayed home."
"Rain, please tell me what that man said on that phone
    was a lie." She sounds angry.
What man?
"Mommy, I'm just not feeling well."
I hear nothing.   I think she's walking out.
            "Rain, are you hurting yourself?"
My heart stops.

I can't breathe
I can't breathe
I can't breathe.
"M-Mommy, 1 . . ."
The covers are pulled from my head,⠀⠀⠀from my
⠀⠀body.
She grabs my wrist.
I'm crying, *"No, Mommy, please! It was an accident!"*
She pushes up the sleeves⠀⠀of my hoodie⠀⠀⠀⠀and sees
all the cuts that paint my arm
like vines, like branches
without roots, without direction.
⠀⠀⠀⠀⠀⠀*"Rain!"* she cries.

Except she's not yelling at me to wake up or to get
⠀⠀dressed.
This is worse. *So much worse.*

⠀⠀Mom pulls me out of the bed and I fall to the floor.

146. FROM THE GROUND

I'm crying the loudest I've ever cried,
but Mommy won't let me go, waiting for me to get up
    from the ground.
"Rain, let's *go!*"
I stand but I don't want to.
"*Mommy*, please!"
She pulls me into the bathroom, opens the cabinet for
    things
to clean my cuts.

She applies the alcohol, and it burns, it burns   *badly.*
  "*No, Mommy! Stop, please stop!*"
  "You're *hurting* yourself, Rain? On *purpose*?!"
  "*No, Mommy, it's not that.*"
She turns me to the mirror.
    "*Look at yourself! Look who you're hurting!*"

I cover my face as I hear Mom walk out.
I slide down on the floor again.
And when I look up from the ground, I see

Xander.

147. I CAN'T

I can't
　　stop my
　　　　body from
　　　　　　shaking from
　　　　　　　　all this
　　　　　　　　　　shame I
　　　　　　　　　　　　feel.

148. MOM HASN'T COME BACK

Mom hasn't come back to see me.

But I can hear her.

She's getting ready for the night shift.

I can hear her even with my head stuffed in my pillow.

149. MY EYES OPEN

My eyes open to a knock on my door.
And I'm scared that it's Mom   again.

"Rain."

My   eyes   open   wide.

Xander.

150. XANDER

Xander comes in, sits on my bed,
wraps his arms around me
and all I can do is cry   in arms so foreign
                                  yet so familiar.
Then he says,
          "Rain, I'm so sorry."
I cry harder.

Then he says,
          "Rain, you can't do this to yourself. I
               need you here more than anything. I
               haven't been showing it lately, I know.
               Everything has been so much, *too* much.
               But please don't hurt yourself. Please.
               I'm sorry for not knowing. I love you so
               much, Rain-drop."

151. FEEL SOMETHING

At school I finally show Dr. McCalla my arm.

I've been in Dr. McCalla's office for hours, but it feels
    like days.

I haven't spoken to Umi or Alyssa or Miss Walia.

I've been here the whole time. He's been asking me
    questions

but they're so hard for me to answer.

Questions about *what's going on with me*   and why I
    think

I do this to myself. I bite my bottom lip.

"I think it started when my dad left when I was little. I
    mean, I don't know, bad things just kept happening.
    Like we were in a shelter and things were really
    hard. And my mom . . . She just slept all the time.
    I mean, she also worked very hard to take care
    of us. I don't know, maybe the thoughts started
    coming before then. Yeah, I think they did. I just
    get these thoughts. I don't know how to explain
    them. It's like, I feel so sad all the time. I feel like
    nobody really loves me. Even when things started

getting better, the sadness never really left. I never
wanted this. I never asked for this. Sometimes it's
so bad I can't breathe and my heart beats really fast.
Sometimes I can't sleep. I get so mad at myself. I just
kept blaming myself. I thought it would be better if
I wasn't around. I think it got worse over the years.
Like I get really anxious. And now my brother is
sad. And my mom's sad again. And it's too much. I
didn't want to fight it anymore, you know?"

Tears start falling and I'm trying to breathe, but I can't.
"Rain, it's okay to cry. Let it out. It's okay to
feel something."

152. IN DR. MCCALLA'S OFFICE

I feel cold all over, because now Mom is here with me.
And so is X.

I can't stop shaking, my whole body is shaking
and I'm playing with my hands
praying   hoping   that this day will end   quickly.

Dr. McCalla tells her about what I'm going through.
He says that he's concerned about things
like *anxiety   chemical imbalance   depression   trauma.*
I feel like   a snowman in the sun.
I look at Mom, whose face I cannot read.
I look at Xander, who looks more like how I'm looking
    and feeling.

> "It also seems," Dr. McCalla continues, "that
> Rain lacks the proper tools to cope with
> the things she deals with in life. And I
> wonder if your family could benefit from
> some type of therapy."

My heart stops.

> *"Therapy?"* Mom's face is still unreadable.

Is she mad? Sad? Will I get in trouble for this?

> "Rain has expressed to me that she's felt
> this way her whole life. Rain has also
> told me about times she thought you
> struggled with sadness. She mentioned
> a time when you would often sleep for
> long stretches of time, when your family
> was living at a shelter. She spoke about
> her inconsistent father during this
> financial hardship. And also about the
> recent incident with Xander. It seems
> as if she's carrying a significant amount
> of suppressed emotional weight. And I

believe your son is carrying this weight
also as the male figure in the house. . . ."

"I was and still am a single mom, Dr.
McCalla. It's not *easy*. . . ." Mom's voice
cracks.

She puts her hands over her face.

"Ma?" X.

"You're right, it wasn't easy. And you're a
hero to these kids. But even the greatest
superheroes need help sometimes, and
that's okay."

Mom begins to cry. X and I wrap our arms around her.

"I'm *so, so* sorry." She cries.

"It's okay, Mommy." My lip shivers.

"Ma, you don't have to say—" X.

"I *want* to."

Dr. McCalla gets up and hands her a box of tissues.

"Let it out," he says. "Let it out."

153. THAT NIGHT

After Mom finally unwraps her arms from around us
    and leaves for work,
I go into Xander's room and sit on his bed. *It's been such*
    a long time since I've done this.
He sits on the other side, his back to me, my back to his.
"I'm not strong, Rain, I'm not." *Huh?*
"Who said you had to be strong? All you gotta be is
    okay."
"But I'm not that either."
I think about what Dr. McCalla said about the
    emotional weight X carries. *We carry.*
"You shouldn't be. Although I've always been jealous of
    how you could hold everything together."
He shakes his head. "Barely. I pretend well." His voice is
    sad but honest. "That night really broke me."
"I know, X. . . . And it's okay to cry. I learned that it's
    okay to feel something."
"You know I hit my head, right? So hard, Rain. All those
    people jumping on me, I thought I was gonna die."

I've tried not to think about it, but all I do is think
about it.

And now X is ready to *talk* about it.

"I know, X." I pause. "Do you think they hurt you like
that because . . ."

"I'm Black?"

"Yeah." I whisper.

"To be honest, I try not to think about it like that. All
that anger builds up when I do, you know? And it's
so *exhausting*. But that's a huge narrative in all of
this. The news, the media, everything. There was a
lot of alcohol involved on their end. It became this
unnecessary brawl. But it's hard not to notice the
obvious, you know what I mean? I *am* Black and got
hurt at a predominantly *white* school."

"That's true."

"Yeah, and trust me, Rain. When it's time, I definitely
get angry and talk my shit—I mean, my *stuff*." He
laughs, and it feels so good to hear it.

"As you should. Especially around Butter, I bet." I laugh.

"You already know." He pauses. "It's sad, though. It
hurts. It hurts a lot. It breaks my heart."

He exhales loudly and I feel it in my chest. It gets silent
for a bit.

"I thought I died. I thought everything I worked so hard
for was in vain. Everything for you, for Ma. Rain, I
was so scared."

I've never heard X speak like this before, and I finally
     feel okay enough to hear it.
To hear *his* truth. X's *x*. The truth I couldn't figure out
     by myself.
Just like how no one could figure out mine.
Tears start falling from my eyes.
"I know, X." He lies down and so do I.
We both lie silently on his bed, looking up at the
     ceiling, as if the stars would make themselves
     visible in our darkness.
"I was almost there, Rain. Everything I did was for
     us. Even things I didn't really care about doing
     anymore." *Didn't care about doing?*
"It's not over, X."
He sighs. "Yeah, I know. I been feeling like a failure.
     Like, how could I be a big brother to you if I can't
     even protect myself?"
"But you didn't do it to yourself. *They* did it to you. And
     X, you ain't gotta be perfect for me or for nobody
     else. I know I'm your little sister, but it's okay to feel
     the way you feel. You're *human*."
I feel like Dr. McCalla.
"You're right." He pauses again. "And you know who
     I called for that night? Who I thought of? To help
     me?"
"Who?"
"Dad."

"*Dad?*"

He laughs lightly. "Yeah, I know. I shocked myself, trust me. Crying out for someone I barely see." He pauses. "You remember how he used to pick me up to take me to the park to practice?"

"Yeah."

"Well, you don't know this but . . . one time, when we went out there, I was getting hassled by these older kids. I was in probably fifth or sixth grade and they were like high school kids, trying to steal my ball and all that. Dad had gone to the store to get some snacks for us. One of them pushed me, I pushed back, and it got them really upset. One of them shoved me into the fence and was about to really tear me up but then all of a sudden, Dad showed up."

"*What?*"

"Yeah, he threatened them, called the cops, and everything. They ran out there so fast. . . . And that memory resurfaced in that moment with those college guys."

I try to remember what I've learned in Circle Group.

"Like a *trigger?*"

"Most definitely, a trigger."

154. I FINALLY GO BACK

I finally go back to Circle Group and say,
  "I've really struggled with some bad
    thoughts. Thoughts that made me hurt
    myself, hate myself on the inside *and*
    outside, thoughts that made me think
    about not . . . living. And now I'm trying
    to learn why. I'm trying to get better."
Tears roll down my nose and cheeks, and even
  more so when Miss Walia says,
    "You guys can support her. If that's okay
    with you, Rain."
I nod and
all of a sudden   everyone is getting up
and coming up to me and giving me hugs
so tight   so warm.
Even Alyssa and Umi
even though I've been such
    a jerk.

    I've never felt so loved.

155. MOST BEAUTIFUL THING

After Circle Group, Umi comes up to me.

"Rain, I'm sorry."

"It's okay, Umi."

"Yeah, but I felt terrible.   I *still* do. Like the worst
    friend."

The look on his face makes me know that he means it.

But the word *friend*   makes me *smile*.

"You were scared. I was too. You helped me."

"Okay, well, as long as we're good?"

"We are, I promise!"

"And you know how you mentioned hating yourself on
    the inside *and* outside?"

I nod, those words still hard to hear.

"Remember, Rain, the most beautiful thing about any
    person is this right here."

He puts his hand over his heart.

I shake my head. "You sound like an old person."

He shrugs. "It's really just straight facts, to be honest.
    That's my grandma's phrase."

I smile. "Come on, Umi, don't get too soft on me now!"
He laughs.
He's right, though.

156. AT HOME

It's a strange sight—Mom and X sitting around the
   dinner table.
But they're here. They watch me eat.
"How was your day?" Mommy asks. "Both of you."
"It wasn't bad," I say.
"It was aiight," says Xander.
But she's not done. "What do you mean, 'it wasn't bad'?"
I almost laugh.
Mom, the dinner psychologist.
"I mean, it was good, Mommy."
Xander grabs Mom's hand. "How are *you* doing, Ma?"
She smiles gently. "I'm good, I'm good, I promise."
She *does* look better. She pulls slightly on my hair.
"I was thinking . . . twists into two puffs tonight?"
I smile. "Sounds good."

157. JOURNAL

It's crazy how much healing can come from just
being honest.

158. STILL DOWN

I walk into Circle Group late and Umi's speaking.
"When my grandma died, it tore me up."
Umi's grandma *died*?
He speaks about her   like she's still alive.
I guess that's how he   *copes*.
Something Dr. McCalla is helping me to do better.

When I'm putting on my coat, Alyssa comes up to me,
    squeezes me real tight,

then pulls out a paper and says, "You still down?"
She puts it in my hand. I look down and see it's the flyer
    for the step team tryouts.
I smile.

159. STEP TRYOUTS

Step tryouts are today and I'm nervous.
Xander says, "Rhythm runs in the family, so you're
    good."
Mom says, "Shine bright like you always do."
Alyssa says, "They ain't got nothing on us!"

It's a lot of people in the gym.
The step coach counts down, "Three, two, one, step!"
and we do what she taught us.
It's fast but I know what to do.
I'm not worried about anyone else   looking at me
                                          judging me
I just follow the beat and go as hard as I can,
giving all that I have,
and it feels *so* good to step again.

160. JOURNAL

Why do we stop doing the things we love to make
others happy?
It felt so good to step again.

161. I NEVER THOUGHT

I have my cell phone up to my face, zooming in on all
    my   flaws.
Trying to accept me for me, but it's hard.
But   *I guess*   my eyes are kind of nice
            my hair kind of pretty   my skin dark and
                    kind of warm-looking,
                                    like a cup of cocoa.
I see some Dad but a lot more of Mom, and Mom is
    beautiful

so that makes me beautiful too   *right?*

"Doing that makes things worse." Xander walks into
    my room.

I drop my phone into my lap.

"You know everyone's got insecurities," he says.

"What could *you* possibly be insecure about?"

I speak before I think   looking up to his face bruised
    with stitches.

He sits. "Everything."

"Everything?"

"If I make it a *thing*, yeah, everything. Look. Give me
    your phone."

I give it to him.

"Look how small my ears look, and my eyelids look
    weird, too."

I laugh.

"No, but for real, Rain. You know what school I go to.
    Only two other people look the way I look. So yeah,
    that makes me insecure at times. It's *real* different
    than going to school here."

"That's true."

"Rain, I'm not the greatest at anything. When I go
    to that school, I'm not the coolest person. I don't
    got the flyest stuff on. Honestly, most times, I'm
    whatever they let me be. Whatever's acceptable."

I never thought of it like that.

I never thought Xander could ever be insecure.   *Never.*

162. WHEN WE WERE YOUNGER

Back-to-school shopping was more like back-to-school
    looking,
but Mom would take X and me with her anyway.
We learned real early in life not to cry for things that
    Mom couldn't afford.
We learned how to have fun window-shopping,
    although deep down
we really wanted some things.
But I hated shopping because it forced me
                                    to acknowledge me.
"You like this, Rain?"
Mom would hold up a shirt. I hated the way tops were
    too tight   or pants were too low
or how workers would suggest I shop in the women's
    section,
where there was no glitter, no butterflies, no rainbows
    on clothing.

"*Women's?!*" Mommy would exclaim, as if I'd been diagnosed with an illness.

I would find a way to escape and find X.

"You know what I do, Rain-drop. I hide them."

My face would scrunch up. "Hide *what*?"

"Hide the stuff that I want so no one buys it. So the next time we come, I can get it."

And that's what we did. We would hide the things X wanted, things I wanted.

And that's what made shopping fun for us, *hiding things for next time.*

163. DR. MCCALLA

I look around Dr. McCalla's office. And I can't believe this place used to scare me.

I've gotten so used to it. I've gotten so used to *talking* to *someone* about my *feelings.*

"So, you've said that you feel like you have to fix issues that affect your family?"

I pick at the granola bar he gave to me earlier.

"Yes."

"But that you don't know *how* to fix them?"

"Yeah." I take a bite of the granola bar. "It's like, I don't know how, but I want to fix them so bad. I get really anxious."

I look down at the paper he gave me with hundreds of different emotions I can use to describe how I feel.

"It . . . ," I begin again. "*Overwhelms* me."

"Can I ask you something, though?"

"Uh-huh." I take another bite of the granola bar.

"Who asked you?"

"Asked me what?"

"To take that on—to fix things?"

"Who *asked me*?"

"Yes, who asked you to fix anything? Like, your mom or anyone?"

"No one asked me to, but—"

"But who *asked* you?"

Wait. I laugh. "Dr. McCalla, nobody, nobody asked me to!"

I get it.

He smiles. "Exactly. So if no one asked you to, then . . ."

"Why do I feel that way?" I try to think,   to *unpack*. Another word Dr. McCalla uses often.

"I mean . . . ," I start. "Xander does it. He goes into this mode to make sure everything's okay for me. And I always felt bad that I couldn't really do the same thing for him."

He's writing things down.

"That's understandable."

"But *who asked me*, right?"

We both smile.

164. THE DOORBELL

The doorbell rings, and I go to the front door.

"Who is it?" I ask.

"It's *me,* girl."

"Alyssa?" I open the door.

"Hey, girl."

She walks in and gives me one of her big hugs.

I'm nervous of what she will think about where I live.

Will she ask where Mom sleeps?

"W-what are you doing here?"

"I don't know. I was kind of bored. Where's your room?!"

"Umm . . . back there. Uh—you can come see if you
    want."

"Yeah, of course!"

I lead her to my room and open the door,

to what feels more like a storage shed than a bedroom

a *girl's* bedroom.

"I like your room!"

Really?

"It's okay."

"You have the cutest teddy bear—oh my
gosh."

She reaches for Mr. Snuggles.

"Nara always called me a baby for having
him all these years."

"Really? I have one just like him."

165. MADE

Alyssa and I go to step practice,   wait to find out if
we've made the team.

Coach is calling names   and she's not smiling.

And she's not making eye contact with me.

And I'm wondering if I should just walk out now.

I look around at all the people in the gym.

Maybe I didn't do as good as I thought.

"Alyssa," she calls.

Alyssa shrieks and goes up to her to get a team shirt.
Alyssa deserves it, she was great. I don't think I—
       "Rain."
Me?
Alyssa shrieks again and I go get my shirt.

I made the team.

166. JOURNAL

I made the team!
I made the team!
I made the team!

167. AT CIRCLE GROUP

At Circle Group,
Miss Walia is handing out journals to use for today's
    activity.
When she comes over to me and I take mine out of my
    book bag   she smiles.
She tells us,
"I want you guys to write down ten things you love
    about yourself."

I open my journal and rub my finger along the lines of
    the page.
            Ten things I love about myself
                is not something I can think of that easily.

168. JOURNAL

10 things I love about myself:
1.

169. I CALL DAD

I call Dad
again.
I was thinking about our trip to the movies
again.
I don't know why I keep on doing it

my cavity.

Tears roll down my face
just as Xander walks through the front door.
"Rain, what's up? What's—"

I wipe my face as quick as I can,   but it's too
    late.   He saw them.
He walks up to me.
                "What's going on?"
I bite my lip.
                "Nothing, X, really, I'm okay."
He raises his eyebrow.
                "Rain, remember we have to be . . ."
                ". . . honest. I know."
I look away as more tears fill my eyes.
X stands there   waiting.   I know he won't just
    walk away.

I cover my face
and lose it.
                "I tried calling Dad."

And then
he holds me.
How Dad should.
How Dad wouldn't.
How X *does*.   Then he says,
                "His rejection is not ours. That's his
                        problem, Rain-drop."
But what really gets me
is when he says,
                "And guess what, Rain-drop? I'm starting to
                        see a counselor at my school too."

170. AT STEP PRACTICE

At step practice
everybody's supercool   and no one mentions
Xander's incident.
There are so many names to remember
but the twins   the co-captains
Tia and Trevor
are the funniest.
                "Let's get it!" Trevor.
                "It's the precision *for me!*" Tia.
We're all clapping and laughing as
different people battle each other.
I'm tempted to join in on it
until Coach comes in.
                "I got something new for y'all," she says with
                a slight smirk.
We all find our spots, and I look over at
     Alyssa   half-excited   half-nervous.
I have to step real hard and
sweat real hard   *in front of other people.*
But no one says anything about it.

It's *step* and sweating is *normal.*
The moves are much quicker   the stomps much
     louder   than the ones from elementary school.
We step standing   we step sitting on the floor
               we clap our hands   we slap each other's
               hands.
Tia shouts,
               "You can't step like us!"
We shout,
               "No way! No how!"
Trevor shouts,
               "Y'all tryna battle?!"
We shout,
               "Right here! Right now!"
Coach pushes us
but she's also real nice.
               "Rain, like *this*!"
She yells   she stands next to me   she shows me.

I follow her lead,
I get it right.
Everybody cheers me on,
And I forget about my worries.

171. DR. MCCALLA

Dr. McCalla asks me,
"Rain, did you ever finish that assignment from Circle
   Group?"
         "Uh, what was that again?"
I'm pretending not to know.
         "The ten things you love about yourself."
         "Oh, yeah."
         "I'll give you some extra time."
Thank God.
         "Okay."

172. JOURNAL

10 things I love about myself:
1.

173. MEAN TO SAY

"Zach's parents wanna invite us to dinner."
Xander jumps onto the sofa   in between Mom and me.
"*Wanna?*" I ask.
"Well, I mean to say, they're inviting us to
        dinner . . . this Saturday."
I look up from my phone.
"Where?"
"Where else? Their house."
I look at Mom, who says,
        "Sounds good to me."

174. GLORY FEELS LIKE

Zach's dad picks us up. His name is Richard or *Rich*.

                                 Go figure.

Xander makes conversation with him the whole time.
I forgot how close X had gotten to Zach's family.

When we get there
Zach and his mom   *Lilian* greet us with hugs and a
    tour of the house.
I stay real quiet.
I'm kind of nervous.
I think Mom is too.
        And I'm trying my hardest not to be mad at Zach.
Their house isn't a mansion.
There isn't a pool.
Zach's room is regular. It looks a lot like X's room.
Actually, I think X's room is a little bit *bigger*.

We sit in the dining room for dinner   for lasagna,
and just like our family

Zach's family is cracking jokes,   and I laugh   like
    real laughter.
Even though I try not to because I'm still upset with
    Zach.
And in good Mom fashion
she talks about church and how good God's been.
Everyone nods.
I haven't seen Mom this happy
in a long time,   which suddenly reminds me that
both of our families have shared similar pain from the
incident.
                Similar but not exactly the same.
Zach gets out this Polaroid camera
and we take a group picture.
Zach's mom   Lilian puts her arm around me and it
    feels okay.
She wants to keep the picture.
            "Look how cute we look, Rain!" She shows
                me the picture.
Cute includes *me*.
            "Take another!" she calls out, and everyone
                laughs.

Zach takes us to his family's basement,
where there's a whole bunch of sports equipment.
I stay close to X and try to avoid eye contact with Zach.

"Why do you have a pink bike?" Xander walks up to it.

X and I start hysterically laughing.

"Hey, hey, chill out, that's my cousin's bike." Zach's face turns red.

"Yeah, sure." X pulls it out. "Rain-drop, you ready for this?"

What?

"What?"

"You ready to ride?"

I wave my hands at him.

"No way, not happening."

"Wait, Rain, you don't know how to ride a bike?" Zach.

I open my eyes wide at Xander.

Why'd he have to say something?

"No. She. Don't."

He brings the bike up to me.

"Oh really? Well, my cousin's helmet and pads are over there."

Xander picks them up and walks over to me.

"You ready, Rain-drop?"

"No, no, no, no."

Is he kidding me?

"Come *on*. Live a little." He puts the helmet on my head. "Put these on."

He hands me the pads.

"But—"

"Come on, Rain. You got me and Xander to
protect you. We're good at that."

He looks me in the eyes and I look away.

"Rain," Zach says.

I keep my eyes down.

"Rain," he says again.

I look up and over to Xander,
then back to him.

"I've said sorry to Xander and your mom so
many times, but I also have to say sorry
to you. If I'm honest, I regret leaving
Xander alone in that situation every
single day. I was afraid and wanted to
get security or campus officers. I felt so
helpless. I know I've disappointed you
and so many others. I'll do whatever I
can to earn your trust. But I know you
probably hate me for it and I completely
understand. You can hate me forever and
I'd understand."

"Okay," I say, because I need time,
and Dr. McCalla says,
That's okay too.

Outside is not as cold because
spring has crept through   without warning   *but*

I like it.

The sun hanging around longer makes me happy.

"Okay now, get on."

Xander and Zach hold the bike.

I'm terrified.

Am I too big for the bike?

"I—umm . . ."

"Don't worry, just get on." Xander.

When I get on,

it's higher than I thought.

"I don't think I can do this."

Zach laughs.

"But you haven't even tried!"

They hold me   and the bike

as I pedal   down the sidewalk   my heart racing.

"Don't let go, *please don't let go*!"

They're laughing.

"Rain, chill out," Xander says. "Remember to

brake, you gotta squeeze the handles."

I nod   but I'm scared.

And we go

up

and down   the sidewalk,

bike wiggling.

"Okay. Rain." Zach. "Now we're gonna let go,

but you have to relax."

"No, no!"

And they let go   and I go for a bit   then I fall.
Then they hold the bike   while I pedal
then they let go   and I fall.
          "You got this, Rain-drop!"
Then they hold the bike   while I pedal again
they let go   and I go for a bit,
and I
keep going
and going
and going.
          "Keep going!" they scream.
and I can't believe
that I'm doing it
and I'm smiling because
                    now I know
                    what glory feels like.

175. AT STEP PRACTICE

Before we step into the gym,
I turn to Alyssa and say,
> "I'm nervous."

She looks at me with widened eyes.
> "Me too. But girl, you're *killing* it. I'm the one
> with the two left feet most times!"

We laugh.
> "No, you're good."

We walk in and are greeted by everyone.
> "Hey, Rain! Hey, Alyssa!"

Coach walks in and we stand in our spots and do our
stretching   and our warm-ups.
My body is aching a bit from our last practice
and practicing every night at home,
but it's worth it.
Coach stands in front of us.
> "Anyone think they have the step from last
> practice perfected?"

My mind flashes back to me in my living room,

stomping,

clapping,

slapping,

moving,

as Xander or Mom play audience and cheer me on.

I look around at everyone.

Should I?

I lift my hand.

       "Rain?" Coach crosses her arms over her

         chest. "Okay, Rain, the floor is yours."

I walk up to where Coach is standing,

facing everyone.

What did I just do?

I exhale   and start.

And although I'm looking in front of me   as I hit

   every move   create every beat

my mind is flashing me back to my living room,

as I stomp,

clap,

slap,

move,

pretending Xander or Mom is the audience and ready to

cheer me on.

        My body   an instrument

          its own   soundtrack.

      Size doesn't matter here but   *sound* does.

I finish and look up
and
everyone starts clapping and cheering.
Alyssa runs up to me,
jumping up and down.   Coach is smiling and says,
            "Who's next?"

176. DRESS SHOPPING

Alyssa comes with Mom
and me to dress shop for the
eighth-grade dance.
We take a bus   to a mall   in another city
and as we walk around
I'm finding it hard to
breathe.
            "How about this store?" Alyssa asks.
She's excited,   way more excited than I could ever be.
            "Looks good to me . . . Rain?" Mom.

I look up at the windows, which are lined with dresses
dresses that I could *never* imagine

myself wearing.

Dresses that look way too expensive.

I wonder if the money Dad gave Mom is enough.

I wonder if he gave her anything at all   *knowing him.*

   "I . . . I guess so."

We walk in and immediately Alyssa and Mom are super
 speeding

     through racks

     and racks

     and racks   of dresses.

I'm walking slowly slightly looking pulling
 at dresses

dreading what's to come next

in the fitting room.

Alyssa comes up to me with too many dresses in
 her arms.

   "You're shopping for you too?"

   "Nope, today's all about you. Plus, I already
    have a dress."

Mom comes up to us, her arms filled with dresses.

   "You ready to try some on?"

   "I guess."

But I'm *not* guessing. I know
 wholeheartedly *I do not want to do this.*

   "All right, let's go!" Alyssa takes the lead,

nearly skipping all the way to the fitting
　　　room.
A lady asks Mom if we need any help.
I shake my head no.
　　　　　"We're fine for now, thank you."
But the lady stays close anyway.　　　Which gives me
　　　even more knots in my stomach.
Alyssa and Mom hang the dresses in the fitting room
　　　for me.
　　　　　"So," Alyssa starts. "Try one on and then
　　　　　　　come out."
I try on a few and they just don't fit right.
　　　　　"Rain, do you need any help?" Mom.
　　　　　"I'm okay," I say through tears of frustration,
looking into a mirror that obviously hates me.
　　　　　"Mommy, if it's too much money, don't . . ."
　　　　　"You're the child. I'm the adult." She pulls a
　　　　　　　dress from the rack. "Don't worry about
　　　　　　　a thing."
Alyssa grabs my hand.
　　　　　"Fight every thought that's telling you you're
　　　　　　　not beautiful, because you are."
She hands me a long blue dress
and I put it on with my eyes closed.
But then I remember Alyssa's words.
Fight every thought that's telling you you're not beautiful,
　　　because you are.

I look straight ahead in the mirror and
admire the pretty dress   as I fight
to see the pretty in the girl wearing it.
But I do look pretty.
I put my hands on my hips.
                    I do look beautiful.
I do a little spin.
                              I think I love this dress.

I take a deep breath.

I'm scared to walk out
but when I do
the saleslady   who just wouldn't go away
says
            "That's the one."

177. LEAD

Step practice has
my thighs black and blue
my arms sore
my clothes soaked in sweat

my hair frizzy
my whole
body
aching,
but Alyssa and I   and everyone else
love it.

> *And people actually like me here.*

After practice
Coach comes up to me and says,
> "Rain, I want you to be one of the lead
>> steppers for our performance during the
>> school district's spring rally."

Me?
I'm not sure
if I can have the students from different schools in my
    City
staring at me.
> "You're doing great," Coach says.
And I'm smiling   I can't stop smiling.

178. JOURNAL

10 things I love about myself:
1.

179. COLLEGES THAT WANTED X

Colleges that wanted X
before the incident
still want him.
But they want to see him play.
"I'm thinking about getting some of my guys
from Elite Prep and City High in some
type of scrimmage game." He takes a
spoonful of his cereal.
Mom's mad about it.

"What are they thinking? That you don't
know how to *play* anymore? That's
ridiculous! Why would they think—"
"They want to see where I'm at physically
and emotionally, Ma. I get it. It makes
sense if they're gonna give me a full ride."

And I'm wondering how long   *the incident*
will linger over our lives.

X gives me a look
that makes me believe
he's wondering the same thing.

180. CIRCLE GROUP

Today at Circle Group
Miss Walia says,
"We're going to go around in a circle and say
I am . . . and use one word about yourself
to finish the sentence. Understood?"
"Yes," everyone says.

They start on the other side of the circle   from
        where I'm sitting.
I close my eyes.
                "I am bold."
                "I am better."
                "I am strong."
                "I am beautiful."
                "I am healthy."
                "I am smart."
                "I am different."
                "I am cooler than cool."
We laugh.
I get so caught up in the words I hear
that I don't realize it's
my turn.
                "Rain?"
                "I am . . . okay."

I open my eyes and Miss Walia is smiling at me.
I smile back because
for the first time
in my life,

                                I mean what I say.

181. AFTER CIRCLE GROUP

Umi asks me,

> "You need a ride to the dance, Rain?"

What?

> "Huh?"
>
> "I mean—uhh, like, my dad could drop us at
> the dance."

I zip my coat up.

> "You, me, and Alyssa?"
>
> "Well, Alyssa's pops is bringing her. So, I
> thought we could go together. Like, if
> you wanted to."
>
> "Oh yeah, that'd be cool."
>
> "Yeah, but like . . . we could also take
> pictures, like, together. If you want; no
> pressure."

Is he—

> "Oh."
>
> "I mean we don't have to."

I smile.

"Of course, Umi. We're gonna be the coolest
ones there."
He laughs and daps me up.
"You already know."

182. PAINT THE CITY

Xander   Dre Dre
Jay   Butter
and Zach
are all planning this football scrimmage   so the
    colleges that
want X   can see him play.

But it's awkward.

Zach was the last one to show up, and it didn't look like
    anyone else knew he was coming.
Or is happy that he did.

        "Wassup, Xander?" He walks in and sits at
            the kitchen table with me

although
everybody else is sitting in the living room.

They look back at him and don't say anything.

     "I want this to be *big*." X breaks the silence.
     "Word, and it will be. Everybody and their
          momma know to show up for this game!"
          Jay.
     "Most def." Butter side-eyes Zach.
Somebody clears their throat.
I pretend to read something in my textbook.
More silence.

     "Listen." Zach stands up from the table and
          walks over to them.
X stands up from the sofa.
     "Zach, it's—"
     "It's cool." Zach turns to the boys. "By the
          way, I'm Zach."
     "Yeah, we definitely know who *you* are."
          Butter's voice is sharp.
Zach sits with them.
     "Listen, X told me he spoke to y'all about
          everything that happened, but I wanted
          to share my side—"
     "What side? There's only one side that

landed our boy in the hospital." Dre Dre.

"Dre . . ." X.

"Nah, it's cool." Zach. "You're right. I wanted to let y'all know that Xander is my closest friend at Elite Prep. That whole fight that happened was originally toward me, but he had my back. I knew in that moment, I couldn't defend him the way I wanted to. I *had* to get help. I'd never intentionally do anything to put Xander in any type of danger or harm. I'm still hurt over the whole situation. I know X spoke to y'all about it, but I really want y'all to hear me out. I also wanted to get Elite Prep involved in helping with the scrimmage to get X where he needs to be come fall. I'll do anything to make sure of that."

It gets silent again.

"To be one hundred percent straight with you," Butter breaks the silence, "I don't trust you. And I don't know how long it'll take. I'm glad you want to help X and you're remorseful and all that, but I don't trust you."

Zach nods.

"I get it, I do."

Jay reaches out his hand.

"Thanks for coming out, though." He daps
Zach.

"Of course."

"We ain't gotta be best friends to get this
scrimmage planned." Dre Dre.

X nods and stands back up and claps his hands together.

"Aiight! So, I have the flyer."

X walks over and hands me the flyers he wants
Alyssa, Umi, and me to put up around the city.

"How big is this gonna be, X?" I ask.

"We're getting players from both City High
and Elite Prep."

My eyes open wide.

"But—"

He nods.

He knows what I'm worried about.

"I know. We're gonna mix the teams up."

I look back at Zach, who nods.

Jay walks over and throws his arm around my shoulder.

"My boy X says he wants to collect donations
to raise money for better uniforms at
City High. He's got some vendors going
out there to sell food and all that."

I shuffle the flyers in my hand and say,

"Okay, let's paint the City then."

183. XANDER'S GAME

Xander has been running around all day
getting things done for the scrimmage game.
I catch him in his room
writing things down.
            "You're good, X?"
I sit on his bed.
            "Yup."
            "How's game prep coming?"
            "Really good, actually. I wish I didn't have to
                play, though."
Huh?
            "Like not in the game or—"
            "Nah, never mind."
He puts his pen and paper down
and rubs his forehead.
            "Are you all right?"
            "Yeah, everything's going well with the
                planning and—"
            "Nah, I mean are *you* okay."

He leans back on his bed.

"You sound like new Ma."

I laugh.

"I know."

"To be honest . . ." He pauses. "Sometimes, most times, I have to remind myself that I'm not where I used to be. Some days I wake up and it feels like the morning after the incident. I feel all that weight again. All that pain. But I have keep reminding myself I'm not there anymore. I've survived that morning and many mornings after that. The scrimmage is a good distraction, but sometimes I just get anxious."

I nod.

"I understand."

"Yeah, and I was speaking to Ma about it. I told her I've been seeing the counselor at my school when I can. And we're trying to set something up so I can see a therapist outside of school too."

"That'll help."

"Yeah."

"Ma said she might see one too."

No way.

"You're lying."

"Nah, for real. Said she was gonna see if her
health insurance would offer her the
option."

"Oh wow."

"Yeah, you know, I was speaking to her.
Being honest, you know? Asked her about
all that sleeping she used to do."

My eyes widen.

"What'd she say?"

"I mean, I'm sure she'll tell you, but she told
me she's been doing it since she was
a little kid. She said before Grandma
passed, Grandma used to do it too, and
Ma sort of just picked it up. She didn't
really know how to talk about hard stuff.
Nobody taught her and she didn't know
how to teach us."

My whole family   getting therapy.
Who would've thought?

184. IT'S GAME DAY

X wasn't lying when he said he was getting
both City High *and* Elite Prep involved.
We're at City High's football field
and I've never seen this many Black and white people
together for the same cause.
The college reps are here.
The local news is here.
The pastor and people from   Hope Church   are here
including Amare and Mrs. and Mr. Porter.
Mr. Jackson   of course   is here.
I even see Willie the barber
who *always* finesses the fade of Xander's high-top.
This is not just for X,
but for our City.

   "I can't believe so many people are here."
    Mom wraps her arm around me.
   "Only X."
   "*Only* X."
Alyssa and Umi walk up the bleachers

to where me and Mom are sitting, with snacks in their
    hands.
                "Yo, this is about to be *elite*!" says Umi.
                "Oh, so you're reppin' *Elite Prep* now?" Alyssa.
                "Nah, I meant the *game's* going to be *elite*,
                    not—"
She hits his shoulder.
                "I know, I'm messing with you!"
We all laugh.
                "The weather's so beautiful today!" Mom
                    says.
It is.
                Extra sunny.
The players start making their way out onto the field
and everyone is screaming,
and I'm screaming so loud
                    and jumping so high
that it feels like I'm going to explode.

And although they mixed both teams
for this game,
Xander still managed to be on the side that's wearing
City High jerseys.

                                        Only X.

185. HOPE

It's the fourth quarter,
the game is tied,
and we're all screaming.

Xander's been killing it and has made
three touchdowns so far and I
keep looking over at the college reps
to see if they like what they see.

There's not enough time left,
and the Elite Prep team,   which includes Jay and Butter,
                                                    yes, *Butter*

has the ball.

          "Come on, X!" Mom screams,
and I look at her and realize
she's sacrificed attending all of X's games
for work.

The Elite quarterback throws the ball
it's in the air

and

Xander intercepts it!

We're screaming!
We're screaming!
Everyone's screaming!

And he runs

and runs

and makes the touchdown.

Both teams are jumping
and cheering
and hugging each other
and with tears in her eyes
Mom grabs my face and says

"There's hope, baby, there's always hope."

186. FANTASTIC FIVE

It's the day after the game and
Dre Dre
Jay
Butter
and Zach are over.

        And I can't stop smiling.

They brought their
game sets and
junk food and
the house is loud   but *good* loud.
Even Zach looks more comfortable than he did last time
treading lightly   still.
And although it's not perfect it's something.

Xander comes into the kitchen to get paper towels.

  "Fantastic Five," I whisper.
  "Huh?"
  "Nothing." I smile. *Nothing at all.*

187. AT CIRCLE GROUP

At Circle Group Miss Walia says to us,
"Remember, *you* are not your *circumstance*."

And I realize that I've never separated the two.

188. JOURNAL

10 things I love about myself:
1.

189. DRESSED FOR THE DANCE

Mom is getting me dressed for the dance,
and I can't believe it's here already.
She bought glittered bobby pins to put in my hair.
She takes the straightening iron out for my hair.
> "I don't want it straight. I want a nice 'fro
> > with the shiny pins."

She puts it down.
> "Great idea."

Mom helps me put on my dress
and my shoes.
She puts a little bit of her makeup on my face.
> "Lipstick?" I ask with my hands in the prayer
> > pose.

She scrunches her eyebrows.
> "Sure, but just this *once*."

I walk out into the living room
fully ready
for the dance.

"You look so beautiful!"
Mom takes her phone out and snaps pictures.
I *never* take pictures
and I'm still feeling insecure
                    but I try to push past those feelings.

I've never felt beautiful before.
"One second," I say, and nearly skip
my way
into the bathroom.
I look at me
really look at me through the mirror.
My dress, my hair, the lipstick against my skin. My *skin*.
My *beautiful brown skin*
like Mom says.
Which reminds me.
I go into my room and find the skin-lightening cream
    stuffed
all the way in the back of one of my drawers.
I tighten the bag it's in and hide it in between my hands
    as I
make my way into the kitchen.
"Rain, you okay?"
"Yes, Mommy."
I stuff it in the trash.
When I walk back into the living room
Xander walks through the front door.

"Okay, Rain-drop, I see you."
I hug him.
Mom is putting on her shoes.
She's leaving before I leave,

for work.

Mom holds my face in her hands.
"Do you know why I named you Rain?"
"Mommy."
"No, really," she starts. "The rain is both
gentle and a force. And that's who you
are, in all things. Be both tonight."

190. KNOCK AT THE DOOR

There's a knock at the door,
and X beats me to it.
He opens it   to a suit-wearing Umi.
"Wassup, man!" Xander.
"Hey, Xander. Hey, R—" He pauses when he
sees me. "Umm, Rain. Hey, Rain."

"Bye, Xander!" I try to walk out the door, but
        he pulls me back in.
"Aiight, so make sure she gets back home on
        time, you feel me?"
"That's no problem." Umi hasn't moved his
        gaze from me. "My dad is taking us and
        picking us back up. Rain will be home on
        time."
"Aiight." Xander turns to me. "Have fun
        tonight. You look absolutely beautiful,
        Rain-drop."
He gives me a hug
and Umi and I walk out.

When we get into his dad's car,   Umi turns to me.
        "He calls you Rain-drop? That's fire—
                I mean, water."
        "Shut up."
I shove him   awkwardly,
because I'm still trying to get comfortable
in this dress   with this makeup.
        "You know my name means something
                similar, right? *Umi* means ocean. So we're
                both like water."
And I'm so excited about that fact   I can barely
        look him in the face.

191. AT THE DANCE

We find Alyssa   *who looks so pretty*
and sit at a table together.

We're at a *hall,*
and the hall is so beautiful that I can't stop looking
     around
at all the chandeliers.
I feel like a chandelier.
We get served dinner on fancy plates.
                         And drinks in fancy glasses.
And this is already one of the best nights of my life.

We're taking pictures   and I actually *like* them.
I like how happy I look in them.

Now everybody is making their way to the dance floor.
I even see Amare out there,
and instead of listening to the thoughts that tell me:

You don't deserve to be here.
You're ugly.
You shouldn't be this happy.
You're not good enough to go out there.
You're not skinny enough to dance.
People are watching you.
People are making fun of you.

I dance   like it's my living room.
I dance   like my life depends it.
And I don't stop   even when
my feet start hurting.

192. NARA

Nara comes up to me
on my way back from the bathroom with Alyssa and
    says in a gentle voice,
        "You look really pretty, Rain."
I pause.
        "Thank you. You do too."

She really does.

She smiles,

I smile,

then we walk away from each other,

and that's okay.

193. AT THE END OF THE NIGHT

Umi and his dad bring me home   as promised.

Umi walks me to my front door.

"Have a good night, Rain-drop."

Then he gives me the best hug that I've ever had in my
life.

194. WHEN I OPEN THE FRONT DOOR

I see X
sitting at the kitchen table   waiting for me
                                                    of course.

          "You're not *tired*?" I roll my eyes,
even though   I'm glad he's up.
The little sister in me   is partly annoyed.
          "Had a good night?"
I kick off my shoes and sit on the sofa.
          "Yup, I'm beat."

He sits down next to me and
I lean my head on his shoulder.
In no time
he's asleep   *my little dad.*

195. THAT NIGHT

I dream of colors,
different colors,
        and I don't know why.

196. BEFORE THE SPRING RALLY

It's the final step practice   before
the spring rally and everybody's hype.
        "I cannot wait!"
        "It's gonna be *crazy*!"
        "So many people are going to be there!"
        "As they should!"
        "My whole family's coming!"
A knot forms in my stomach.
I feel   *panic.*

I start taking the deep breaths I learned in Circle Group.

In through the nose,
out through the mouth.

"Rain, you okay?" Alyssa.
I nod and then she starts breathing with me.
"Y'all good over here?" Trevor.
He walks up to us   we nod   then he starts
    breathing with us.
Soon
everyone is walking over and breathing with us
    until the final   exhale.
"That was calming. I needed that!" Tia.
I nod.
"Same."

197. DR. MCCALLA

Dr. McCalla says,
"Remember there's validity in how you feel.
Your feelings are valid. They are not
stupid."

"Yeah, but—"

"Say it."

I sigh   in frustration   but in relief.

"My feelings are valid."

198. REALLY MADE OF

I tie the laces on the black combat boots I have to wear
for the step performance,

       then walk into the bathroom   and look at
          myself in the mirror.

      "At ease, soldier." Xander salutes me,

       trying to look serious   but smiling anyway.

I   push   him   out   of   my   mirror view.

      "Camo's cool." I pause. "Especially with this."

I turn around   with my back to the

   mirror   looking over my shoulder.

My name is printed on the back of my shirt: *RAIN*

I smile at how cool it looks   it *feels*.

We both walk out of the bathroom.

"How you getting there?"

      "Bus. I'm meeting up with Alyssa." I pause.

"You're coming, right?"

"Of course. But don't be shocked if they call
me up there. I'm pretty talented. Look
how good I can snap."

I push his hands, laughing.

"Please stop before the ash on your hands
starts a fire."

He laughs.

"Aiight then, you better show them what
you're *really* made of. Not some rain
shower. Bring that Rain-storm."

199. THE ONLY PERSON

Walking down the halls of City High with the team
brings back so many memories.
Xander would practice   and play   here
when he was younger.
Nothing much has changed.

Same lockers.   Same walls.

"I'm so excited!" Alyssa throws her arm
around my shoulder.

"Me too!" And I am.   *Or at least I'm trying
         my best*
     to feel   something other than   anxiety.
We walk into the gym
and it's *so* packed.   We hurry off to the side.
Coach calls all of us steppers   into a circle
     holding hands.
          "Now ladies . . . fellas . . . don't be nervous.
               You guys have practiced really hard and
               will do really great. . . ."
I feel her eyes right on me when she says,
          "The only person that can stop you—is you."

200. THE SAME THING

It's finally our time to step   and we all march out like
                                        soldiers,
get into formation
          with music   and a smoke machine.

My heart is beating real fast,
as I march to the front of the line.

It feels like everyone in the gym is staring at me,
I'm trying to remember that   *there's nothing to be
    afraid of.*
I look up at the top of the bleachers and see waving
    hands,
Xander   Mom   Miss Walia.

                              I didn't expect them
but I'm so glad they're here.
                    I open my mouth.
        "Y'all ready?!"
The crowd is screaming
probably wondering   *who's this girl in front of us?*
or rather
who has she become?
Sometimes I wonder the same thing.

                                        I got this.

201. WHEN WE GET HOME

X gets his speaker because it's a celebration.
        "Baby, you did so well." Mom squeezes me
           planting kisses on my head like
              seeds in a garden.
  Part of me worries about the sacrifice she made to see
                      my performance.
Part of me can't stop smiling because she came anyway.
        "Come on, y'all!"
Music starts blasting from X's speaker and
he switches the music to Afrobeat
hip-hop
salsa
jazz
        just about anything to keep us *moving*.

Mom does a shimmy move with her shoulders and
X and I look at each other and
burst out laughing.   Then we try it.

We're laughing and pretending like
we're in some old-school movie,
or at some family reunion–type thing with a
soul-train line.

All of me
doesn't want this night to end.

202. I HAVE A DREAM

I have a dream
of different colors
        red   purple   blue
        green   white   yellow
          moving moving moving fast
              waving waving waving fast.

203. NORMAL

After school
I sit at Miss Walia's desk   because she lets me,
so I staple papers together for her   while she does
    her grading.
Sometimes she lets me help her grade   *a privilege*
not many kids get.
A sign of trust   some would say   *extra work*
but it makes me feel special.

> "You're doing good in your classes?" she asks
>   without looking up.

I nod.

> "Yes, ma'am."
> "And graduation's coming . . . how are you
>   feeling about that?"

I look at her   seeking an answer   seeking
    reassurance   but to be honest
I haven't thought much about it.

> "I'm not sure yet. Kind of nervous, kind of
>   scared."

She looks at me and smiles.
    "That's normal."

204. DURING CHURCH

Girls and boys come out   in flowy white-and-purple
    outfits,
and they're waving flags
of different colors.

            Red   purple   blue
            green   white   yellow,
                moving moving moving fast
                    waving waving waving fast.

And I feel this *peace*.
        And although the flags wave fast
there's a stillness   to it.
And the colors   are *beautiful*.

After church   I find Sade,
the dance leader,
who carries flags under her arms,

who I've known most of my life,
        and say,
           "I want to flag . . . I don't know if I'll be good
                at it, but—"
She touches my shoulder.
        "You'll be great."

205. MATH FINAL

Xander is helping me study
for my math final,   *and I hate it.*

        "Do the first three problems on this page,"
           he says,
and I sigh, but try it.

Miss Walia says
sometimes the things we avoid
are the things we need in order to get better.

206. FLAG PRACTICE

I walk into Hope Church for flag practice and I know
about half the kids in the room.
There are little kids   preteens   teens   and
    even some adults.
All of them
              waving
                      different-colored flags
                                      around.
          "Rain!" Sade comes up to me.
Unlike Sundays—
her hair is tied up and she's wearing sweats.
I wave.
          "Welcome!" She squeezes me tightly. "I'm so
              glad you're here. Are you excited?"
Her smile is so wide   I swear it could stretch across the
    whole city.
              "Y-yeah, I am." I pause. "To be honest, I'm a
                  bit nervous."
              "I completely understand. I'll be walking
                  around and assisting everyone. But I'll

send over the teacher you'll be working
with today."

So, it's not you?

"It's not—" I begin, but she walks off.

I take my coat off and put it on the back of a chair.

It's hot in here and my nerves are making me even
more hot.

"Rain?"

I know that voice.

I turn around and it's Amare   holding two flags
under his arm.

"*Amare?*" I suddenly remember why I'm here.

"Wait—you *flag?*"

He rolls his eyes.

"Yes."

I laugh.

"Nah, no judgment, but like, I had no idea.
I'm *shocked.*"

"Everyone says that. I'm not really loud about
it." He hands me one of the flags.

"Wait, you're my *teacher?*"

I'm laughing again.

He exhales.

"*Yes*, Rain."

"But I've never seen you perform." I unravel
the flag a bit.

"I'm a little more behind the scenes. I haven't

performed in front of others yet."
"Why?"
He shakes his head.
"Stage fright."
"You?"
"Yeah, me. Why *not* me? Everybody's
got something."
Everybody's got something.
"Okay, then show me what you got." I smile.
And without music
Amare unravels his red-and-orange silk flag
waves it and moves his body in such a way
that leaves me   speechless.
Like karate meeting ballet. Both elegant and strong.
Is this Amare?
When he stops   I can't stop clapping.
"Amare . . . *Wow!*"
He smiles and bows.
"Thank you, thank you. It's one of those
gifts that I didn't ask for."
We both laugh.
"You're really good."
"Thank you. Now unravel yours."
I look around at everyone else with their flags, then
slowly unravel the sheer, silvery-blue flag
in my hands.
"It's beautiful."

"It is." He nods.

I look over at a girl I know named Sana,

who's waving the flag slowly over her head, and I   do
    the same.

"So, Rain, you steppin' *and* flaggin'? What's
    got into you?"

"What do you mean?"

"Can I be honest?"

There goes that word again.   *Honest.*

"Yeah."

"I've known you since we were little and I
    ain't never seen you outside of Nara's
    shadow."

Ouch.

"*Dang*, Amare."

"Nah, nah, I mean, it's a good thing!"

"I mean—you're not *wrong.* I'm just going
    through some changes, you know?"

He nods.

"I'm happy for you. Honest, Rain."

My eyes water a bit.

"Thank you." I pause. "How is she, though?
    Nara."

He shrugs.

"She's cool. Dante and Nara are always
    chillin', never worried about much."

I laugh.

"You're right about that."

He lifts his flag up in the air.

"Aiight, so you're ready?"

I nod.

He smiles.

"Follow my lead."

207. KNOW-HOW

X has me outside playing catch with him

in the street   like the old days but

his arm is something *serious*.

I dodge the football, which is coming at me at   full
    speed.

"I can't catch those!"

He laughs.

"And why not? You're my sister. You can do
        anything!"

"Anything?"

"Real talk, Rain-drop!"

I pick up the ball and throw it back.

"How's counseling going?" I ask.

He throws it back.

>"It's solid. It's going pretty good."
>
>"That's good."

I throw it back.

>"It made me realize that I kind of knew, you
>know, about your sadness."
>
>"Oh yeah?"

He throws it back.

>"Yeah . . . that's why when we were younger,
>I'd always try to take you to the park . . .
>to my practices . . . wherever. I just never
>said anything."

I freeze mid-throw.

>"Why wouldn't you say anything?"
>
>"Chill, Rain, don't get uptight about it."
>
>"I'm not. . . . But why, why didn't you ever say
>anything?"
>
>"The same reason you didn't. I just didn't
>know how."

208. CELEBRATING

I never like celebrating
my birthday,
born in spring   hence Rain.
X in the summer   Mom's sunshine baby.

        I never thought I deserved a birthday
           a celebration of *me*.

209. BIRTHDAY

Today's my birthday,
        what X calls *May-Day*,
and Mom invited Alyssa and Umi over.
We're in the middle of eating cake and
Alyssa hands me a gift bag   with balloons on

it   and yellow tissue paper on the inside.

     "From me and Umi." She smiles.

I look up at Umi, whose smile makes me look away.

I reach in   and take out something black   black cloth,

a flowy black dress with yellow sunflowers all over it.

     "Oh, this is beautiful, Rain," says Mom.

I hold it up to my body.

       "I love it! Thanks, you guys!" I hug it against

        me.

       "Rain waters flowers," says Alyssa.

       "And then they grow." Umi pauses. "And

        then *we* grow."

And then we grow.

210. DECIDED

X wants to tell me and Mom something
and I'm nervous.

He tells us to sit around the kitchen table
while he stands,   pacing.

"Xander, what's going on?"

Mom's impatient *like me.*

"It's about college."

My chest starts hurting.

"What about it?" I ask.

He exhales.

"Ma, please hear me out, all right?"

Mom folds her arms across her chest.

"I'll hear you out if you tell me what's going
on."

He sits down at the table.

"Look, I love sports. I love what being an
athlete has done for me, but I'm not sure
if I want to continue in that world."

Mom scrunches her eyebrows.

"What are you talking about?"

He pauses and exhales.

"I've decided that I'm going to be rejecting any sports
scholarship and not playing college sports at all."

211. NEITHER OF THOSE

Mom slams her hand down on the kitchen table.

>"*What?!* Xander Washington, how will we
>afford your college tuition?"

"Xander, you can't do that," I say.

>"Ma, I *have* to. I'm tired of going back and
>forth in my mind. I learned so much
>after the incident. People see me and
>they think all I've accomplished is
>because of sports, and that's not the case.
>I'm smart, Ma, *real* smart, and y'all know
>that. But the world just sees another
>body. Another Black body for pain or
>entertainment, and I want to be neither
>of those."

"Who cares what the world thinks, X?"

>"I know, but deep inside of me . . . I just—"

He pulls out a stack of envelopes.

>"These are schools willing to pay my
>tuition based on my grades, Ma. *Full*
>scholarships without sports. I never

wanted to do sports forever."

He hands Mom the envelopes, and she looks through
   them.

She exhales.

   "Are you sure this is what you want to do?"

   "Positive."

   "But don't you love playing?" I ask.

He exhales.

   "I do. And I love how far it brought me. But I
      can't carry that weight in college. I really
      want to focus on my studies without fear
      of injury. But I'll always play for fun and
      use it to relieve stress when I need to."

The look on Xander's face tells me that he's serious.

   "What do you want to study?" I ask.

I realize that I've never asked about the *study*
   part   always
the sports
the scouts
the *division*.

   "Psychology and sociology. Maybe get into
      psychiatry."

My mind thinks back to all the times I found Xander
   reading his textbooks about the mind
for *fun*.

How could I have missed it?

   How could I have missed *him*?

"Okay." Mom pauses, then smiles. "I support
any decision you make. My son, the
doctor."
Mom gives him the biggest hug
and I can't help but smile   as Xander's face looks
    relieved   he looks

                                                    free.

212. FLAG PRACTICE

I'm back at flag practice and
my arms are sore.
Today Amare isn't here, but I've got the same flag and
Sade is teaching me.
        "Okay, Rain, how about we take a little
            break?" Sade says.
I put the flag on the ground and walk with her over to
    the snack table.
I sit and she sits across from me.
I grab a small bag of mixed nuts and a bottle of water.

"How would you feel about performing?" she
      asks.

I take a drink of water.

    "Umm . . . *me?*"

I look around at everyone practicing and they look
   so   happy.

Even though I love   to flag

I'm not sure   if I'm as good as the others   yet.

    "Yup, you."

Too many thoughts flood my mind at once.

    "Like, performing in the church? I don't
         know. I have some things going on. I
         know at church it's a little different. I
         don't want to be fake, but I'm not always
         happy and all that. Flaggers usually look
         so happy and giddy. And I'm in therapy
         and stuff and—"

    "Rain, I'm not looking for performers, I'm
         looking for real. And everything you're
         saying confirms to me that you're perfect
         for this. Think about it?"

    "I'll think about it."

213. TOGETHER

Today
Umi
Alyssa
and I get our caps and gowns.

I walk around my home in mine.

The next day
Xander gets his cap and gown.

He walks around in his too.

We will experience something bittersweet
but *together*.

214. FINAL

Today is the math final,
and I'm so nervous.
   "You got this, Rain-drop. Remember, you're a
     Washington."
But when he says that,
I think of Dad and wonder
if he was good at math like how X is.

215. LAST MEETING

In my last meeting with Dr. McCalla, he asks me,
   "How are the thoughts?"
   "Better."
He raises his eyebrows at me in slight suspicion,
and I get it,

I really get it.

Because I lied before   and there's no telling if I'll
    ever lie again.

"I'm serious," I say with a little smile, because
        I wouldn't believe me either.

But I *do* believe me.

If I didn't,

I wouldn't be okay.

I'd never get better.

"Your mom and I have been talking about
    your next steps. In regard to therapy.
    And in making sure you regularly see a
    counselor at City High once you start in
    September."

"Yeah, I know."

"Also." He pauses. "Do you have it?"

"It took me a long time to even think of
    anything."

I open my book bag and take out my journal and hand
    it to him to read.

216. JOURNAL

10 things I love about myself:

1. My heart.
2. My (new) ability to be honest about how I feel.
3. I'm forgiving, or I try to be, although it can be hard.
4. That I'm hardworking in school, step, and flag.
5. I'm funny sometimes.
6. I'm smart, although I do struggle in math.
7. My kindness.
8. My beauty (which I admit I still do struggle with).
9. I think I can be a fun person (when I'm comfortable).
10. That I have the capability to grow, to learn, to change, to get better.

217. **PROGRESS**

Dr. McCalla reads my list   smiling.

    "This is really good, Rain. Remember, in
        everything, progress, not . . ."
    "Perfection," I say with him.

218. **THE LAST DAY OF CIRCLE GROUP**

Today's the last day of Circle Group
and it's a party.

There's food and music
and everyone's laughing   *but I feel so sad, because it*
   feels like everything's

                 ending.

"Everyone, everyone!" Miss Walia claps her
hands. "Go around, hug somebody, tell
them that they're great and don't stop
until you've hugged everyone!"

And now I can't stop smiling.

219. CITY HIGH PROM

Xander is going to City High's prom
and he's wearing a fly deep blue suit,
and his date is in a beautiful blue dress.

Dre Dre
Jay
and Butter are with their dates and
looking *oh* so *Hollywood.*

Mom and I are outside, snapping pictures in front of a
    limo
with other families   *and even Zach.*

This is like a dream to all of us.

220, WAITING

I wait
for hours
and hours
for X to come home   from prom.
But the wait is just way too long
and I'm dozing off every five minutes.

The door closes.
I jump out of my sleep.
      "X?"
I wipe my eyes.
      "Oh, so you're my mom now?"
I laugh.
      "Yeah, let me smell your breath."
      "Rain, chill out," he laughs.
      "How was it?"
      "It was . . . man, it was home. I didn't realize
         how much I missed everybody I grew up
         with. It may not be Elite Prep, but home
         is home. Best night of my life."

He sits down next to me.

I lean my head on his shoulder.

In no time

he's asleep   *my little dad.*

221. XANDER'S GRADUATION

Today is Xander's graduation, and I don't know exactly
    what I'm   feeling.

I watch   as Mom gets dressed in her Sunday
    best   for her baby,

her Xander,

our Xander's big day.

She stands in front of me   in her nicest blouse and
    slacks.

        "How do I look?" she asks.

Mom has never been one for affirmations, so I know
    she's nervous.

        "You look really pretty."

She kisses my forehead.

        "You too, my darling."

I'm wearing the sunflower dress   that I got for my
        birthday.

We're getting a ride from Zach's dad   *Rich*,
and the car ride is not awkward like last time,
        but   joyous.

The graduation is *huge*
and when they call Xander's name,
the whole place erupts.
Because it's
Xander
aka X
aka Xceptional X
aka Xcellent X
the best X-ample   who's *a low-key hero* in our   City,

                        and anywhere else he goes.

222. THE RECEPTION

At Xander's graduation reception,
a cameraman captures Xander
putting his graduation cap and gown on me.
        "You're next, little sis."

223. JOURNAL

I can't believe I'm really graduating!
Or that X graduated!
Everything is happening so fast. . . .

224. RESULTS

I get my math final back,
and it's a pass.

"But it's a seventy!" I complain to X.
"Listen, it's a pass and you worked hard."

He gives me a high five
and I take some time
to be proud of me.

225. RAIN RISING

Amare is back and we've been rehearsing with the flags
   for hours.

"Why does this feel harder than stepping?"
Amare laughs.
He's teaching me choreography because I told Sade that
   I would perform if
I could get it right.
If.

"Sometimes"—he waves his red-and-orange
   flag—"you have to put life into your flag
   to experience it better."
"What do you mean?"
"I mean . . ." He begins waving his flag
   rapidly. "To me, my flag represents fire.
   The red and orange. And fire spreads
   fast. Fire is consuming. And that's how
   I wave it. I wave it like I have fire in my
   hands. What do you feel like your flag
   represents?"
I look down at the sheer, silvery blue in my hand.

"Not trying to be funny or nothing, but it
      reminds me of the rain. The sheer of it.
      The silver. And the hint of blue reminds
      me of how rain feels. Rain always feels
      kind of blue to me, even on sunny days."
"Okay, so show me motions of the rain."
I wave the flag up, then downward slowly, then fast.
      "What about if there's wind?" he asks.
I turn in circles with the flag out in front   of me.
      "Now what about the unexpected?"
The unexpected?
I stop moving.
      "What do you mean?"
      "Sade taught me this. What is something
      that the rain *doesn't* do, but that *we* can
      do through flaggin'?"
I wave my arms upward.
      "It doesn't go upward. It doesn't rise like
      this."
I keep waving it up and around.
      "So now you got rain rising." Amare.
      "Rain rising," I repeat. "Rain rising."

226. GRADUATION DAY

Today is my graduation,
and I realize that
I'm cool with more people than I thought.

I'm taking pictures with people from the step team
and
Circle Group
keeping   Alyssa and Umi close by my side.

I can't breathe.
I can't breathe.
This doesn't feel real.

                                        I exhale.

As we line up for our names to be called
            to receive our promotion certificates,
Alyssa squeezes my hand and says,
"You got this, girl!"

And then they do it,   *they call me.*
                "Rain Washington."

And there's more applause for me than I thought there
        would be.

Miss Walia comes up to me and I hug her
for what feels like hours.
                "Rain!" She wipes my tears away with her
                        hands. "You're stunning."
I hug her some more.

Dr. McCalla comes up to our family and says,
                "As you guys continue to grow, to heal, make
                        sure you replace the broken areas with
                        good things, or they just remain empty.
                        Replace sorrow with the things you love."

Then he high-fives me.

And Mr. Jackson,
vice principal,
football coach,
Xander's #1 fan

                        runs up to X at *my* graduation
                congratulating *him* on *his* accomplishments.
But all I can do is laugh.

227. ALYSSA'S FAMILY

Alyssa's family is throwing her a graduation party.
And this time
instead of sitting in the corner,
I dance with them,
I sing with them,
I laugh with them.

> "We have to promise," Alyssa says to me and
> Umi.
> "To hang out this summer before we get to
> high school."
> "Bet." Umi.
> "Definitely."

228. EXACTLY WHAT I NEED

I'm lying on my bed
tears streaming down my face,
                    when there's a knock at the door.
It's X's knock.
            "Rain, you okay?"
I bite my bottom lip.
I don't know what to say.   *I'm kind of ashamed for*
        feeling this way.

                                For still struggling like this.
            "Want something to drink?"
I don't answer, but
he comes back with a cup of warm milk.
I sit up and sip from it.
He gets on the bed.
            "Aiight, so you drink up and I'll lie down
                    right here if you're ever ready to talk."

And for now,
that's exactly what I need.

Progress, not perfection.

229. TRUTH

It feels just like how my dream feels except   this is *real*.
I'm wearing a long, flowy blue dress   and in my
    hands
are two sheer, silvery-blue flags,
and I'm waving and spinning.
And although I'm at church,
                                I feel like I'm in heaven.

I look and see Xander and Mom smiling so wide,
and as the music plays,   I feel brave,
                                I feel free,
                                I feel like rain.
I feel like Rain.

                Rain rising

                                through the unexpected.
        Gentle and a force   like Mom says.
        I feel like me.

AUTHOR'S NOTE

For most of my life, I felt ashamed to be sensitive. I lived with a big, sensitive, easily wounded heart in a world that wasn't so gentle. I grew up believing survival was more important than my emotions, which isn't true. I became what you could call an "emotional stuffer." I stuffed all my feelings on the inside, thinking that there was nowhere for me to let them out. That no one would see me or hear me. That no one would understand. Or that I'd get in trouble for feeling the way I felt.

I remember the day when the voice of a little girl told me about this big brother of hers. He was her hero. He was her safe space in her times of sadness. A sadness she often didn't understand. I knew this little girl was little me, crying out to be heard. Crying out for that safe space. I knew there were a lot of young people crying out for the same thing.

I knew I had to write her story, my story, our story.

Reader, I know how important it is to talk to somebody about how you feel. Even if you feel ashamed or feel like you're being a bother.

Plot twist: You're not a bother, and you shouldn't feel any shame.

Your feelings really *do* matter.

And no matter what, you are *so* loved.

And despite what you're going through, imagine yourself as beautifully crafted clay that can bend and break but can be molded back together again, even more beautiful. This is what Rain had to learn, and this is what we must always remember.

Reader, *Rain Rising* is my gift to you. Let's laugh, cry, dance, heal, and rise together.

Always together.

ACKNOWLEDGMENTS

First and foremost: "Holy Spirit, activate! Holy Spirit, activate!" Thank You, Jesus, for saving me, loving me, and cementing gold in between my broken "cracks" for the greater good. Thank You for carrying me and my family through dark days and for being the ultimate Healer. Thank You for hope, unspeakable. Thank You for purpose. Thank You for the gift of words. You are so faithful in every season. Grateful that "I am who You say I am" even amidst the trauma, the depression, and the anxiety. Thank You for new beginnings at what looks like the end.

Thank you to my soul mates: my mommy, Tetlah Teresa Stewart Comrie, may this book be a direct reflection of all your sacrifices. You did it, Ma. It wasn't easy, but you did it. Thank you for being our real-life superhero; we love and appreciate you so much, Mama ToTo! I'M A PUBLISHED AUTHOR, MA! My sisters, Alisia "Lisa / Lee Lee" Allen and Toni "TT" Comrie, my bestie boos, I love and need y'all always. God really blessed me with you two. Thank you for the laughs, the tears, the hugs, and the support. Thank you for all your talents that have inspired me to be the creative that I am. Thank you for being the best sisters a girl could ask for. Julanie "JuJu" McCalla, Savannah "Sammy" Fisher, and Gordon "GG" Gaston, you all make life worth living. My inspirations. My gifts. CoCo loves you all so, so much. You are all so smart, so amazing, so beautiful, and so talented. I'm so blessed to be your auntie and will always be there for you!

Thank you to my wonderful agent-author, Rena Rossner, for believing in this story. I still can't believe it. Thank you for being the coolest and kindest agent ever. My editor, Alyson Day, you are the best! Thank you for literally everything in this publishing process. For making me feel seen and inspired. Also, thank you to Eva Lynch-Comer, the copyeditors, and the entire HarperCollins team that had a hand in Rain's story coming to life. Thank you all so much.

Thank you to Dhipinder "Rosie" Walia, aka Walz (Queen Walz, to be exact): my real-life Miss Walia. Thank you for being the brilliant professor, writer, and creative human that you are. Thank you for caring for your students the way you do. Thank you for always looking out for me. Thank you for teaching me, pushing me, and believing in me. Thank you for believing in this story and my story. Thank you for a being such a bright star amidst dark memories. Thank you for making me feel like me. What a gift to have you in my life. I love you so much, sister.

Thank you to Sade Bailey-Lombardi, circle-time extraordinaire and fabulously fierce educator. Love you, girl. Justine Hale, who taught me "Who asked you?"—which I'm still working on, I promise. My family's own little dad and big bro, Shannon "Bobby" Gordon: we love you. Lawrence Kevin Patterson, for always building me up as a person and an artist: love you, Pop. Geevanesam "G" Devakanmalai, for the unpacking, reflecting, and poetry: I love you. Antoinique Abraham and Elizabeth Anoff, the time capsules of all the school memories: love you both.

Shout-out to the loveliest students from the Bronx and Mount Vernon, New York, who inspire me, who I'm rooting for. Love you all.

To those who play a consistent, positive, encouraging role in my life: you know who you are. Big thanks and big love, always.